The WRONG MAN

Norma Iris Pagan Morales

ISBN 978-1-959895-90-9 (paperback)
ISBN 978-1-959895-89-3 (ebook)

Printed in the United States of America

DEDICATION

This novel is dedicated to my beloved sister, ADELIN MILAGROS PAGAN MORALES. She is gone; however, she still lives in my heart.

Contents

CHAPTER 1

David Meeting Johnny

"I said I'm here to see my son, David said, standing firm in the doorway.

Delia tried to slam the door on his face, but he stopped her by putting his foot out so she couldn't shut it.

Her heart pounded in her ears. No. He couldn't. He wouldn't! She pressed on the door with all her weight but it wouldn't move.

You didn't want to have anything to do with him when you found out I was expecting. Why are you interested now? She said.

He's my son. He pushed the door open and stormed past her. She ran after him as he walked down the hallway of the boarding house.

You can't do this! He ignored her and opened the kitchen door. Get out of here! Delia demanded.

You can't keep me from him, Delia, he said as he paced toward the four-year-old boy who stopped eating his soup.

Delia gave Mrs. Diaz an apologetic look as she raced to the small round kitchen table and put her hands protectively on her son's shoulders. You're not taking him, David. I won't let you!

Johnny looked at David but didn't say anything.

Smiling at the boy, David knelt in front of him. Good morning, Johnny, I'm your dad.

Delia's gaze shifted from David to Mrs. Diaz who set down the stack of newspapers and gave her a questioning look.

Delia silently pleaded with her landlady to help her. Turning back to David, she said, you can't do this.

His cold brown eyes met hers. Delia, I believe I have a right to my own flesh and blood. He pulled out a chair and sat on it so he could be eye level with the boy.

Now, Johnny, I hope your ma told you something about me.

Johnny looked up at her. Is he, my pa?

Taking a deep breath, she debated how to answer his question. All David did was make it possible for her to conceive the child. She hardly considered him a real father. Who would have thought five minutes could change everything?

Ma? Yes.

The confirmation tore at her heart. She knew the day might come when she'd have to reveal the truth of his family but hoped it would be when he was older, when he could fully understand the situation.

David shook his head at her. You didn't mention me at all?

She gritted her teeth. You weren't around.

He smiled at Johnny. Your pa had some important business to do. I'm done now, and you and your ma will come with me to New York.

We will not! Out of the corner of her eye, she watched as Mrs. Diaz quietly left the room. Her grip on Johnny's shoulders tightened.

Come on, Delia, David argued. Be reasonable.

Our home is here. We're not leaving, and we're certainly not leaving with you.

Johnny needs a father.

You didn't think so five years ago. I was wrong. He attempted to rest his hand on hers, but she pulled away from him as if his touch burned her.

People make mistakes, and I made a horrible one. I intend to be a part of your life.

No! Scared, she grabbed Johnny from his chair and picked him up. Holding him close to her, she rushed toward the kitchen door.

David blocked her exit. You're not going anywhere. He's my son and I have every right to talk to him.

Despite her shaky hands, she refused to back down. You gave up those rights when you abandoned us.

He threw his hands up in the air. I had to get settled. I didn't have the money to support you and a child.

You hopped on the first train out of here. You said it was my fault I got in the family way. You even said someone else could be his father.

Shrugging, he stepped toward them. How could I say that you weren't sleeping around with other men?

Anger swept through her. How dare he! Could he easily forget that he took her virginity? Used goods. That's all I am and that's all I'll ever be. However, it wasn't time for regrets. She had to protect her son.

I know Johnny is mine. He took another step closer to her. I want to do right by you and him.

No, no you don't.

She didn't trust him. Something was wrong. After five years, he showed up at the boarding house and asked her to marry him.

She refused, figuring she was better off continuing on as she was rather than condemning her life to a man who left when she needed him most. And now he was threatening to take Johnny from her!

Standing in front of him, holding an overwhelmed little boy, she refused to move.

What is the problem? he demanded, anger creeping into his voice.

She nearly cried with relief when Sheriff Rodriguez and Mrs. Diaz entered the kitchen.

Is there something I can help you with, Mr. Jimenez? the sheriff asked. He straightened his vest, causing sunlight to bounce off his shiny badge.

David faced him, his hands relaxing at his sides. Hello Sheriff. His tone cordial, he smiled. I'm just saying hi to Delia and my son.

Oh, Sheriff, don't you believe him for a minute. Mrs. Diaz slipped between Delia and David.

She's been asking him to leave but he won't.

Sheriff Rodriguez looked at Delia.

Is that true, ma'am?

Forcing her tears back, she nodded. Yes, sir. I don't want him here.

Turning to David, he said, "This is a personal residence. You must leave."

A father has a right to talk to his son, doesn't he? David asked.

You must consider the mother's thoughts on that. I'd say you have to wait until she's willing.

His mouth formed a thin line. We'll see about that. He stormed out of the kitchen, letting the front door bang shut behind him.

Delia exhaled, unaware that she'd been holding her breath.

Mrs. Diaz gave her a hug. You don't have to worry about a thing. You have family and friends who are here to help you.

Thank you, Maria. She let Johnny stand on his feet.

Though her son looked puzzled, she decided she would talk to him later. She needed time to think. David's arrival had been unexpected.

The sheriff led Johnny back to his soup before urging Delia to the other side of the room. Resting one hand on the worktable and the other on his hip, he whispered, "I don't think he'll stay away. I've dealt with this before, and some men can get persistent."

She folded her hands together, squeezing them. "That's what I'm afraid of. Sheriff, from the way it sounded, he wants to take Johnny away. He can't do that, can he?"

There have been kidnappings. Her stomach knotted up, making her feel queasy. She glanced at her son who hadn't touched his food. Though he didn't fully understand what happened, he knew it wasn't good.

Never once did she imagine David would return, much less want his son.

What should she do? Maria asked.

He stared at the floor for a good moment before he said, A married woman has an easier time than one when it comes to certain men coming around uninvited.

Marriage? She long since gave up on the idea of getting married when she discovered her pregnancy and David bailed on her.

A man would provide a stable environment for a family.

He'd be the protector if David returns. Men like David tend to stay away when there's another man around.

She sighed in despair. The sheriff was right. David ran from her brothers when they searched for him and he just backed off when the sheriff came, so she knew he'd back down when confronted by another man. She failed to be intimidating enough to make him leave.

No reputable man will marry me, she replied. In fact, single men avoided her because of the stigma associated with her.

I have a new deputy who's due to arrive in September.

He rubbed his chin. His name is Irving Santos, and he'd probably be willing to take a wife. He's one of my cousins.

Since he can't have children, no woman's been interested in him. But you have Johnny already, and he won't mind the fact that the boy's not his.

But won't his reputation suffer for it?

I've been told that Irving is a force to be reckoned with.

He doesn't care what others think. He's tough as nails and strong as steel. A few rumors won't bother him.

Feeling overwhelmed, she rested her head in her hands.

This is happening too fast.

First, David shows up and now the sheriff's trying to pair me up with his distant relative. I can't process all of this at once.

I'll tell you what. The man cleared his throat and stood up straight, making her look his way.

I'll send him a letter and see what he thinks. We still have two months before he arrives.

That should be plenty of time for the two of you to make a decision. Nothing must be done today.

She closed her eyes for a moment, glad that she had time to think.

What do we do about David in the meantime? Maria wondered.

Keep Johnny in this house. If Johnny is here, David has no right to intrude on your property.

Why can't you just arrest him?

On what grounds? He hasn't committed a crime.

She groaned. I know you're right, Sheriff, but I don't like it. Alright. Off with you. The poor boy and his mother need to calm down.

As Mrs. Diaz screamed him out, Delia murmured her thanks, and looked at her son.

His eyes met hers and tears formed in her eyes. Spinning on her heel, she reached for a clean washcloth to wipe her wet cheeks. I don't know what to do. Though it was true that she didn't have to plan today, she didn't want David coming back.

She saw the determination in his eyes. He wanted Jeremy for something, and whatever that something was, there was no way it could be good.

Owen Russell held the cards firmly in his grip. Play it calm. You're almost there. He eyed the money in the center of the round table.

After seven hours of playing poker, it all came down to this moment.

If I win this hand, Aunt Rachel will be financially stable again. The dim light in the saloon and the heavy smoke gave him a headache but he pressed forward. He hated being here. But he had to do this. If he didn't, his aunt would end up homeless.

Ignoring the drunk patrons and the prostitutes lingering around, he straightened in his chair and focused on the cards in front of him.

Forcing his attention from the whispers as people bet on who would win, he peaked at the clock. Almost five in the morning. Almost there. Just be calm. This game was very important.

Out of the eight players who started the game, only he and Big Roy Hawke were left. A quick glance at Big Roy, aptly named for his overweight frame, notified him that the bearded, dirty man worried that he'd lose his money.

Though Big Roy prided himself on his ability to bluff, he had a habit of chewing his toothpick faster when he didn't have a good hand, just as other players had their own subtle cues that told Owen when to raise the ante and when to fold. In this case, Owen had raised the stake.

The remaining sum of his aunt's life savings sat in that sizable pile of coins in front of him.

Owen slowly exhaled, willing his fingers steady so he couldn't grab the stash and run. He had to play it cool. He studied his cards again, just to make sure he had a possible winning hand.

The royal flush stared back at him, the charming diamonds and clovers seeming to dance in tune with his heartbeat.

I call. Big Roy's gruff voice interrupted the murmurs around them. He shoved his remaining money forward.

Downing his shot of whiskey, he glared at Owen. What'd you got, boy? Without bravado, he laid his cards on the table.

Diamond King, Queen, and Jack with Clover Ace and King. Big Roy swore and threw his cards on the table. He had been holding three of a kind.

Loud shouts and harsh pats on Owen's back from the men who bet for him brought him to his senses. He did it! He got his aunt's money back! Accepting the bag, the bartender handed him, he collected the money, hoping he didn't look too eager. He needed to act like he did this kind of thing all the time.

Unsure of what the winner usually did but not wishing to offend the bartender who'd been kind to him, he gave the man a tip and headed out. He bypassed several prostitutes who flirted with him and left the establishment. He breathed a sigh of relief. Thank goodness.

He never wanted to go into another place like that ever again! With the adrenaline rushing through him, Owen took his horse and rode the steed hard until he arrived at his aunt's small wooden shack that rested along the swamp.

He couldn't wait to see her face when he showed her the money! He anxiously knocked on the door.

One glance at the light filtering through the canopy of trees surrounding the house told him it was dawn. This would wake her up, but it was for a good reason. He knocked again, this time making his rapping louder.

He heard the creaking of the floorboards as she shuffled to the closed door. Who is it?

It's me, Aunt Rachel, he said.

Owen? She opened the door, surprise written on her face. Come on in, son.

He did as she bid and entered her kitchen that didn't have room for more than two chairs and a wobbly table.

She hastened to make a pot of coffee while he set his bag of winnings on the table. How is that fishing business of yours doing?

Great. I got two new customers last week. Sitting in his usual spot, he took his ratty hat and put it on the table. He ran his hand through his light blond wavy hair. I'm sorry I woke you. I know you like to sleep until nine.

She waved her hand. I always have time for my favorite nephew.

I'm your only nephew.

That doesn't stop you from being my favorite. She set the pot on the old cookstove. The open window allowed fresh air in, and though no breeze wafted in, it did serve to cool the place down at night.

He chuckled. Why don't you sit and talk? He leaned forward, his elbows resting gently on the table in case he knocked it over.

I'm coming. She turned and froze in place. Eyebrows furrowed, she shot him a curious look with the same blue eyes he and his father shared with her. You haven't been misbehaving', have you?

Look before you jump to conclusions. Boy, you'll send me to an early grave if you've been misbehaving.

I only set things right for you.

Not looking convinced, she gingerly opened the brown sack, her jaw dropping when she saw the money inside.

Oh Lord, he's fallen in his uncle's footsteps. Her words choked on a threatening sob.

I'm not going back there, Aunt Rachel. I made enough to gain back the savings Uncle Jim lost gambling. That's why I went. Now, I want you to move out of here and get a good home like you always wanted. I promise I won't gamble again.

Her lower lip trembling, she sorted through the cash.

Owen, I... Breaking off, she reached across the table and gave him a big hug and kiss on the forehead. It was a foolish thing you did, but I'm glad you did it.

He returned her hug and laughed. Now, don't spend it all in one place.

She playfully slapped him on the arm and settled into her chair.

Alright. Since you saved me from the poor house, the least I can do is feed you. Are you hungry for biscuits and eggs?

His stomach rumbled. I sure am. No one makes biscuits as tasty as you do.

Then you just sit back and relax. I'll have your meal ready soon. He put his hands behind his head and enjoyed their easygoing conversation for the rest of the morning.

CHAPTER 2

The Cronies

Owen was leaving the bait shop to go fishing at sunrise when he saw Big Roy's two cronies, Michael, and Lenny, walking toward him.

Despite the six men who lingered inside, talking, and laughing, and the old man crossing the street from the pier to the shop, he felt isolated.

He recognized the twin rail-thin brothers from the saloon. By the looks on their faces, he knew that they meant business...and that business was him. Without waiting for them to catch up to him, he bolted down the street.

Come back here!

As if I'm that stupid! Owen didn't bother glancing back as he raced passed an elderly couple and a small group of men. A dog jumped in front of him, barking, and he tumbled, his fishing supplies flying out of his hands.

He quickly debated picking them up, but the sound of eagerly approaching footsteps behind him made up his mind. Scrambling to his feet, he turned the corner of a street and ducked into an alley. He found a large dumpster and huddled behind it.

Taking deep breaths to calm the pounding in his heart, he focused on the sounds around him. He heard the click-clack of horses as they made their way down the street and the chitter chatter of women.

He didn't hear Big Roy or his goons. That was a good sign. That meant they didn't know where he was. He'd lost them. Just to be extra sure, he waited a good five minutes before he felt safe enough to emerge from his hiding place.

Took you long enough to get out of there. Owen jerked. Lenny and Michael had been waiting for him on the other side of the dumpster. Lenny was smiling at him as he rubbed his new beard with a knife.

Stupid, Owen. You should know to examine all your surroundings!

Without thinking, he ran down the alley, aware that the two men were in close pursuit. The wind blew trash around his feet, but he hardly noticed the wreckage.

He was quickly approaching a well-traveled street. If he could make it there, then Lenny and Michael would have to back off since they couldn't afford to be seen trying to kill someone.

Big Roy had trouble with the law, and one more mess would be his undoing.

Owen was only five meters away from the street when Michael jumped on him and knocked him to the ground.

Grunting, he dodged the knife in Michael's hand and quickly pushed him away so, he could jump up. He took out his own knife and waited for one of the two men to make their move.

This wasn't good. It wasn't good at all! He'd never been in a fatal encounter in his entire life. If only he could get out of this...alive.

If you would just reimburse Big Roy the money you stole from him, then you wouldn't have to run.

Lenny spit the tobacco he'd been chewing onto the ground.

Do they know about Rachel? The last thing his aunt needed was these men tracking her down.

Just take us to the bank where you deposited the money or show us your little hiding place for the cash and we'll let you go, Lenny continued, his grin showing off his yellow teeth.

Owen breathed a sigh of thanks for the small fortune in knowing his aunt was safe.

Where's the money? Michael snapped.

He forced the man's words to make sense over the loud pounding in his ears. His heartbeat with a nervous dread. He wasn't strong enough to fight both. He knew it. He was about to die. But he decided that if he was going to die, then he'd die fighting, even if it did scare him.

Give us the money, Michael ordered.

I don't have it, Owen replied. I lost it in another game. If he could take their mind off his aunt, then his death would be worth it.

How could you have done something that stupid? Lenny hissed.

I got greedy, he explained, though in the back of his mind, he knew it was pointless to do so. I had no idea my opponent was cheating.

Too bad for you that we don't believe you, Michael sneered. Someone as smart as you wouldn't be done in by a cheater.

He wasn't sure which man dove at him first, but he stuck out his knife and plunged it into Michael's gut. He let go of his weapon and fought against Lenny who got behind him and wrapped his arm around his throat. Owen backed up and rammed into a wall.

The force of the impact caused Lenny to let go of him. Glancing down at Michael, he realized that he had mortally wounded the skinny man. Though Michael was still breathing, he wouldn't be much longer.

Lenny glanced at Owen for a moment in disbelief. Owen took Lenny's hesitation and ran for the street.

Just as he reached the brick road, a horse whinnied at him, startling him.

The driver of the buggy stopped the horse.

He killed my brother! Lenny pointed an accusing finger at Owen. Murderer!

This caused a great upset from the people watching them, and a marshal called out for Owen to stop.

Before he considered the fact that running only made things look worse, Owen took off down the street.

He managed to lose the marshal and get to his small home where he grabbed his horse and ran the poor animal out of town. He didn't have a destination in mind. He just rode north.

Sandy held Delia's hand as they sat on the bench at the park and watched their sons play. Delia hadn't slept a wink in nearly a week, and she desired her pounding headache to go away.

This couldn't be happening. It was like a nightmare. David had been roaming around the place and following her and Johnny ever since that day he'd asked her to marry him. She knew he was using her to get Johnny.

Why should he care so much about Johnny now? Why? After all this time? She closed her eyes, determined that she wouldn't cry.

Delia swallowed the lump in her throat and looked away from the two laughing boys who threw a rubber ball back and forth.

I don't know what else to do but find a husband. Sandy shook her head in dismay.

Do you have any idea why he wants to be a father suddenly? I keep telling you no.

Sandy squeezed her hand. I'm sorry. Forcing a smile, she patted her hand. Thank you for being here through all of this.

What are sisters for?

A round of laughter coming from David brought Delia's attention to him.

She stiffened. He was strolling through the park with his mother and pointing at Johnny, as if he had any right!

He glanced at her and turned to say something to his mother before he walked over to them.

She briefly noted Sandy's sharp intake of breath as he knelt in front of her. Pressing her back to the bench, Delia shifted as far from him as possible. Though she was a grown woman of twenty-two, he made her feel as if she were a child.

I'm willing to be reasonable about this, he smoothly stated.

All you have to do is marry me, and I can do right by our son.

No, she firmly stated despite her trembling hands. It's not fair to keep a man from his boy, Delia.

It's also not fair to leave an expectant mother to fend for herself, Sandy snapped.

Now, you get away from here before I hit you with my purse. I'd like to see you try. David smiled, as if enjoying the possibility.

Is there a problem here? the sheriff asked as he quickly approached the bench.

David jerked to his feet and cleared his throat. Without a glance in the other man's direction, he scampered back to his mother.

The sheriff sighed. I can see that he's as bad as I feared.

Are you alright, ma'am?

Delia nodded, even as a flush of anger and frustration warmed her cheeks. She hated this.

She hated how David refused to go away. Rubbing her eyes, she desired herself to remain strong.

I have good news, he said, unfolding a letter he'd been holding.

Owen was leaving the bait shop to go fishing. That's good because we could use some fish, Sandy replied, letting go of Delia's hand so she could hug her.

David won't leave her alone.

I just got word today that Irving is in Tennessee. He says he'll marry you.

He handed Delia the letter which she took in shaky hands. He's riding horseback out here with his goods as we speak. I didn't read the part he wrote to you, but I read enough to know he'll be here by October 1st.

The knots twisting in her stomach nearly overwhelmed her. She glanced at David as he continued to watch Johnny. The sooner, the better.

Keep praying. He turned and headed in David's direction to suggest David and his mother move along and enjoy the nice day, which they finally did.

I hope that Irving is as big and strong as the sheriff claims, Sandy muttered, crossing her arms.

I can't believe David his mother. Delia turned her attention to the letter so she could read it.

Delia,

Forgive my delay. I had a last-minute run in with some bandits in South Carolina. They have been apprehended. I proceed west. I agree to marry you. You should know that it is physically impossible for me to consummate our relationship.

There was a showdown I had ten years ago with an unruly young man. I lived through it, but it left me unable to conceive children. I will give Johnny my name and protection.

You don't need to worry about that. I think over time we might be good friends.

Signed,
Irving

It wasn't a love letter, but Delia was hardly in the position to be taking suitors. What she needed was a husband and he volunteered to be one so she could keep David away.

It's enough. After all, that's all a woman like me can hope for. Sighing, she closed her eyes, once again wishing she had done things differently five years ago.

As much as she loved her son, she mourned the fact that she hadn't waited to get married before she had him. If she had, then she wouldn't be in this situation right now.

But she couldn't live in a world of if only's. She'd marry Irving and be glad for the favor he was doing her. She wouldn't concern herself with childhood fantasies of love. Love had no place in doing what was best for her and her son.

Never look back. Keep moving forward.

Don't look back. Keep going forward. Owen rode his poor horse so hard that it finally stopped in the middle of a forest, not caring that its owner poked it in the sides with his spur on.

Wiping the sweat off his forehead, Owen wearily set the hat back on his head. His blond hair was matted down with sweat and his three-week-old beard lined his jaw.

He spied a river close by, so he slipped from the horse and gasped. Being on a horse for almost three weeks made his entire body stiff, especially in the saddle area.

He tied the horse's reigns to the tree before he waddled to the shore of the river which dipped out of sight from the place his horse stood.

He cupped his hand in the cool water and brought the refreshing liquid to mouth. Water never tasted so good!

Deciding to take a swim to wash nearly a month's worth of grime off his body, he eagerly threw off his clothes and dipped into the water.

Though it chilled him, he couldn't recall a time when he felt better. He really was lucky that he got out of Louisiana alive.

He washed his body off the best he could. At least, he felt much better. Dipping into the water for another drink, he paused when he heard a gunshot. Tensing, he stilled his swimming as he listened to his horse's neighing.

Another gunshot silenced the animal. He winced. Poor Charlie. He loved that horse.

That's his horse alright. After a moment's pause and snapping twigs, the man said, I want him alive.

Owen would have recognized Big Roy's gruff voice anywhere. How did he find me? He passed through so many forests, he thought for sure he'd lost the intimidating gambler.

I want to kill him for what he did to Michael, Lenny said.

You'll get your chance, but no one harms a hair on his head until I deal with him.

Though Lenny grumbled, he didn't protest.

Owen tried not to make any sudden movements as he slowly made his way to the shore. He gingerly stepped on the dry soil and rushed behind one of the many trees in the vicinity, glad he swam far enough from his horse to avoid being seen by the three men who crowded around Big Roy and Lenny.

The trees hid the moonlight, making his task of hiding easier. He had to figure a way out of there. But how? He didn't have his horse anymore. He glanced over his shoulder and caught sight of a campfire in the distance.

Perhaps he could enlist help?

He shook his head. The last thing he wanted to do was involve an innocent party into this mess.

Maybe the man would be willing to give him some clothing and a ride into Nashville. Liking the idea, he cautiously made his way to the fire. When he reached the spot, he frowned, realizing that the man had left his bedroll to go off somewhere, probably to take care of personal business.

Boss, there's a fire up ahead! Lenny yelled.

Though Lenny was still far enough away to not spot Owen. Owen didn't want to risk being found.

He frowned at the thought of stealing another man's clothes but saw little choice as the five men ran in his direction.

He sorted through the traveling bag and pulled out a large brown shirt, long black pants, and leather boots.

The clothes were too long and loose but he wasn't in the mood to be picky. He shoved a brown hat on his head and shuffled his way to the horse that was tied to a tree.

Flinching at the realization that he had to steal the horse, he quickly threw the saddle and bridle on and jumped on the animal.

What do you think you're doing? A tall man with a hefty build emerged from the trees, pulling up the pants of his longjohns.

I'm sorry. I don't have a choice, he hastily whispered.

Who's there? Big Roy yelled, his Voileses. Frightened, Owen fled from the site. The last thing he heard as he maneuvered the steed through the maze of trees was the tall man saying, Well, well...If it isn't Big Roy and his men.

Interesting running into you here. What that meant, Owen didn't know, nor did he care to find out. He kept moving. He made it to Nashville and snuck aboard a supply car on the train, hoping he succeeded in evading the group for good.

CHAPTER 3

Meeting Owen

Owen entered the restaurant, aware of the looks he was getting.

Oh well. He'd just have to act like he didn't notice the snickers.

He was lucky to even be alive. Taking a deep breath to steady his nerves, he found a seat in the corner of the spacious room and sat down. The boots that were much too big for him scraped across the hardwood floor.

He had to pull up his pants so they didn't fall. Rope. He needed rope. Or a belt. But then, a pair of pants that fit would do even better.

He took a deep breath and allowed himself to relax. He made it to Omaha. That meant his problems were finally over.

No one would be looking for him this far out west.

What can I get you? a woman wearing an apron asked, holding a pad and pencil in her hands.

Right. Food. He quickly picked up the piece of paper in front of him and read the list of menu items. Do you have any fish?

She grinned. No. We don't. Hey, you sound funny.

You aren't from here, are you?

Well, I just love the way you southern men talk. It's adorable. He stopped himself from rolling his eyes. Great. Just what he wanted to be: adorable. Clearing his throat, he said, I'll start with a cup of coffee please.

You're so polite too! she squealed in obvious delight before she skipped off past the other patrons who filled the place.

He took off the hat that was too big for his head and placed it beside him on the table.

Leaning back in his chair and closing his eyes, he gave himself permission to relax. His muscles loosened and the beating of his heart slowed to a normal pace.

Now he'd get a good meal, find a place to stay, and shave this horrible bush off his face. He hated beards. He didn't understand why other men wore them.

They itched and food got stuck to them. He rubbed his jaw, the irritating beard scraping his fingers.

Get a shave. Maybe he could go to the barber. He dug his hand into the pocket of his pants and pulled out the coins. He hadn't realized the man had pocketed some money in his pants when he took the clothes.

As bad as he felt about spending it, he didn't see that he had much of a choice. It wasn't like he could repay the man, so what did it matter at this point? Hopefully, the man would be compensated somehow.

Here you go, the woman sweetly spoke.

He opened his eyes and straightened in his chair. Thank you.

Have you decided on what you want to eat?

Yes. I'll have the pork chops.

A wise choice. Barry isn't in the kitchen today.

His eyes widened. Whatever did that mean?

She walked off before he could ask. He grimaced. It was better that he didn't know. He pulled out a napkin and folded it. As he did, he scanned the room, checking the group of about fifty people who assembled tables remained vacant.

That was just as well. He could blend into the background better in a crowded room.

A man wandered past him and joined what looked to be his friends at the table close by. He sat down and picked up a glass of water.

Well, David, the man across from him began, it's almost October 1.

September 29, he replied, lifting his glass and chuckling.

Here's to October 1st.

Here, here, another man said.

Owen wondered what was so important to the four men but decided it didn't matter. He took a scoop of sugar and put it into his coffee before he stirred it.

Lifting his eyes, he caught sight of his reflection in the mirror on the other side of the wall.

Maybe he'd get a haircut while he was getting the shave.

You know, she should be glad I came here to do the right thing, David said. I don't understand what her problem is.

Maybe you shouldn't have left to begin with, one of the others replied.

Come on. I wasn't ready for the responsibility back then.

Tell us the truth, David. Why do you really want to go through with this?

I told you. To do the right thing.

I don't know, another man spoke up. Maybe you should give up.

Are you kidding? I must get my boy.

The waitress returned with a plate full of pork chops, a baked potato and beans. Here you go, you adorable thing you.

How old you are, son?

Owen debated whether to answer her. After all, that didn't seem to be any of her business, but since she oversaw his food, he figured he better oblige her.

Twenty-four. He picked up the cup and took a drink of the hot liquid. Into the restaurant at the noon hour.

He figured that only two Ooh! You know, I have a daughter who just turned nineteen. Why, you two would make such a fine-looking couple, and you know, she can't resist a southern gentleman.

He nearly spit out the coffee he was drinking.

Too bad she doesn't like bearded men. She patted him on the shoulder. Don't be a stranger.

He touched his beard. Maybe he should keep it on. He didn't exactly relishes the prospect of women trying to fix him up with their daughters, especially women who thought he was adorable'. Adorable was for puppies and kittens, not grown men.

The men in the table next to him got up, threw some money on the table, and left the restaurant.

Owen watched them through the window as they walked down the street, laughing like a bunch of idiots. He didn't know the specifics of what David wanted with the woman they talked about, but he felt sorry for her. He hoped she didn't give into him on whatever it was he planned for October 1st.

Forcing aside the thought, he ate his meal.

After he paid the bill, he pulled up the pants by the belt loops and held onto them as he meandered down the boardwalk, wondering if he should make a home here in Omaha.

The town looked like it was thriving. It was so different from Louisiana.

The air wasn't as humid, and he felt a chill that he usually didn't experience until December. Did they get snow this far up north?

He shrugged, supposing he'd find out if he stuck around. Several people cast odd looks in his direction, and a couple of women giggled as they scurried by him. He sighed.

First things first; he'd go ahead and get that shave and haircut and then get new clothes. Then he could decide on whether to make this his new home.

He found the barber shop and got the shave and cut. His blond hair no longer fell over his eyes, which was a good thing.

At least he could see clearly. He rubbed his jaw. Now that the itchy beard was gone, he kind of missed it.

For some reason, he felt naked without it. But he knew that sensation would pass.

As he searched the businesses lining the street, he caught sight of a Wanted: Dead or Alive poster. He halted in mid-step, causing someone to bump into him.

Sorry, he mumbled to the man and stepped forward, so he was out of other people's way.

He studied the poster. Alright. So maybe the shave was a big mistake. He tried to determine if the drawing looked like him enough for someone to recognize him.

His name was right there for the world to see. "Owen Russell" was under the drawing of his face in bold letters. Under his name was written "Wanted for Murder".

The queasy feeling in his stomach threatened to upset his lunch. Wow. This really wasn't good. How had word spread about him anyway?

He lowered the hat over his eyes and hastened down the boardwalk, hoping no one realized that the man in the Wanted poster was him. Yes, he had murdered Michael, but it had been to defend himself.

How did the sheriff in this town know about that anyway? Big Roy. He must have sent his cronies out to spread the word about me. It made sense. Since they couldn't get him, they figured they'd frame him.

Great. If the sheriff in this town knew Owen was a wanted man, then chances were good that no matter where he went, he'd run into other sheriffs who knew the same thing.

Except if he ended up in a small town. He quickly pulled out some of the change from his pocket. Did he have enough to get to the end of the world? That might be far enough.

Now, hold it right there, someone said from behind him.

He gasped and raised his hands, dropping the coins which rolled on the boardwalk and settled several feet away from him.

He'd been found!

This was it. He knew what happened to men accused of murder. They were hanged. God, I'm too young to die!

The man chuckled. Very funny, Irving. You can put your hands down. He reluctantly turned around and winced at the older man who had graying hair and a gun in his holster. The sunlight bounced off his shiny sheriff badge, as if mocking him. He lowered his hands, but only slightly.

The man frowned and took a step closer, his badge still flashing in the sunlight. You look familiar. Have I seen you before?

Owen's eyes darted to the Wanted poster that was not even five feet from them. Did that drawing look just like him?

He decided to hedge his bets. No. I don't think so.

Hmm... The man closed the gap between them and took off his hat. Hey!

The man held up his hand to quiet him. He looked at the inside of the hat and a big grin crossed his face. Irving Santos.

It is you! Your ma said that you always put this design on your hat. He pointed to the deputy badge that had been stitched into the front of the hat.

Owen nearly fainted with relief. Thank goodness! The sheriff thought he was someone else. Well, that was easy enough.

He'd play along and then get the heck out of town. He laughed and pulled up his pants which had slipped to his hips. You caught me. I'm Irving.

I haven't seen your ma since we were kids. Had it not been for your hat, I wouldn't have recognized you.

I'll be sure to tell her you said hi.

He turned to run off, but the sheriff grabbed his arm. Do I look like a fool.

Owen swallowed the lump in his throat. No, sir.

Then why are you playing me for one?

Alright. So, the sheriff knew he had lied about being Irving. I can explain. You see, I have this aunt.

Right. My ma. We're cousins, and your ma assured me that you were the best deputy back in the Carolinas.

The...the Carolinas? Your aunt? My aunt? Our mothers? Now he didn't know what was going on. Was this good or bad or what?

I'm glad you finally got here, Irving. We sure do need a good deputy around here who can do his job. I had to let the last one go because he hit the bottle too many times.

He put his arm around Owen's shoulders and walked with him down the boardwalk.

I must admit that I expected you to be taller though. You look weak. Didn't that mother of yours feed you anything?

Before Owen could answer, he laughed and patted him on the back. Must be all that running you do after the criminals.

Well, don't worry. We'll get you set up soon enough and you'll have a woman who'll cook all your meals for you.

Owen wanted to ask what he was talking about, but the sheriff stopped.

The first thing we need is to get you into clothes that fit.

You can't be fighting the law in clothes that are ready to fall off you.

Fighting law? he dumbly asked.

Oh, Irving. You're such a kidder. Come on in.

Owen slowly entered the store where a thin man worked on setting up the belt display by the window.

Hi there, Ernie! This here is my cousin, Irving Spencer.

He finally arrived. The sheriff turned to Owen. I got to admit, we were starting to fear you weren't going to show.

We? Owen asked.

Ernie laughed and motioned to Owen. What a hoot!

The poor boy needs clothes alright. And fast.

That's my thinking on it as well, the sheriff agreed.

We'll start him up with two pairs of pants, four shirts, two belts, your best pair of boots, and a better hat than this one. He tossed the hat in the trash can.

Looking at Owen, he said, no offense, son, but you must have a hat that fits right on your head.

You know, Meyer, I must admit that your kin look younger than I thought he'd be.

Sheriff Meyer looked Owen up and down. I thought you'd be older too. Just how old are you anyway?

Uh... Did Owen dare tell the truth? How much could he afford to play into this game before he could slip out and escape town?

Finally, he decided that he couldn't tell too many lies. Besides, would it matter once he hopped another train to get out of here? Twenty-four.

I don't know why I thought you were in your thirties.

The sheriff shrugged. No matter. We'll get you settled in and then you can start your job.

My...my job? Owen wiped his forehead and stared at the moisture on his hand. Man, was he ever breaking into a sweat!

This was worse than sitting in that godforsaken saloon. But not as bad as being chased by Michael and Lenny.

Still, there was that Wanted poster outside. He gulped the nervous lump in his throat. The sooner he got out of town, the better off he'd be.

The sheriff laughed. You're my deputy. He patted Owen on the back, nearly knocking him over. Boy, you need to get some meat on those bones. I don't know why I thought you were built like a brick wall.

Apparently, your ma exaggerated some things about you in her last letter.

Owen grinned and shrugged. What else could he do? For all he knew, Irving was a tough man. Then he remembered the man who owned the clothes he was now wearing. His eyes nearly popped out of his head. Was that Irving? The man was like a might oak!

Anyway, Meyer continued, waving in Ernie's direction, go get measured and we'll get you set up. I'm going to get some people together and we can get the ball rolling on things.

Things? Owen asked, his mind taken off the large man in the forest. What things?

The sheriff left without answering.

He groaned. He needed to get out of here! As he made his way to the door, Ernie stopped him. Not yet, Mr. Spencer.

We must get you in decent clothes first. Now, if you'll follow me over to the mirrors, we'll get started.

Owen glanced at the door, biting his lower lip. Well, he might as well get a good set of clothes. Then he wouldn't stick out like a sore thumb. He checked the change in his pocket. At least he wouldn't have to rip off poor Ernie.

Alright, he finally consented and followed the man to the back of the store.

CHAPTER 4

Waiting

Delia stared at the calendar on the wall in the parlor. It was September 29th and Irving hadn't arrived in town yet.

She glanced at Johnny who played jacks with Sandy's son, six-year-old Greg.

One-year-old Isaac sat in the corner of the room and chewed on a stuffed toy.

Delia looked over at her sister who didn't say anything, which was unusual for her. Then her gaze shifted to Mary, her sister-in-law, who was the mother of Isaac.

She usually enjoyed her time together with her two closest friends. But she couldn't today.

Irving said he'd be here before October 1st in that letter, didn't he? Mary asked, as if she could read her mind.

Delia exhaled and rubbed her temples, willing her headache to ease. That's what he said.

He does have tomorrow to show up. Mary's voice drifted off.

The silence hung heavy in the room. What could any of them say? Irving probably wasn't coming.

Delia took a deep breath and clenched her hands together.

Maybe I should marry David. Sandy gasped. Don't you dare!

But I can't fight him forever. Besides, maybe she was being selfish in keeping Johnny away from his father.

We'll get our brothers to chase David out of town, Sandy insisted, banging her hand on the arm of her chair.

It worked before, and it'll work again.

Steve's ready to go after him. Tom and Joel are too, Mary added.

And don't forget Richard. Why do I think even my husband will have a go at that no good...

Sandy shook her head, obviously biting back the word she really wanted to use that no good man!

David has his brothers with him this time, Delia argued.

And he's not trying to avoid being a father.

Sandy huffed. Well, we have more brothers than he does.

Greg and Johnny laughed as the rubber ball bounced across the floor. Greg ran after it and brought it back to the set of jacks lying on the floor.

Delia wiped her eyes. How she wished that David would stay away, but he wouldn't and she was tired.

The excited knocking at the door startled her.

I'll get it, Mary said as she stood up.

It's not October yet, Sandy whispered. Keep praying, Delia.

Don't give up hope.

I've got good news! a male voice called out.

Delia turned her attention to the sheriff who looked like he was ready to throw his hat up in the air and shout for joy. Her pulse sped up and she jumped from her seat so she could run over to him.

Is Irving here? Please say yes!

Just came in off the train, he replied with a big smile and a nod.

Sandy and Mary hugged her, but she was too busy asking the sheriff to repeat himself to pay attention to them.

He came just in the nick of time, Sheriff Meyer assured her. He's getting ready for the wedding as we speak.

Oh, you should put on your best dress, Sandy squealed.

I love weddings!

I'll watch the children while you get ready, Mary said, grinning. You two go on upstairs.

I'll go tell the judge to get ready with the vows, the sheriff responded.

Make sure to get Judge Johnson, Sandy stated.

Delia rolled her eyes. I don't care if your husband does the wedding or not. I just want to get married.

She turned to the sheriff. Whoever is available will be fine.

She watched in part amusement and part frustration as Sandy mouthed the words Judge Johnson to the lawman. Then her sister ushered her up the stairs.

Owen studied his reflection in the mirror. The dark blue pants, crisp white shirt, and dark blue vest was nice, but he wondered why Ernie felt the need to give him a suit when a pair of denims and the shirt would have done just fine.

Ernie patted him on the shoulder. You look elegant, Mr. Spencer. Why, I hardly believe you're the same man who came into my store!

I can't believe it either. Owen touched his chest. Yes, it was him alright, but he'd never worn a suit in his entire life. It just didn't look like him.

Here's your suit jacket.

Wow. This must be expensive. He touched the fabric before he slipped it on.

Don't worry about it. The sheriff's paying.

What? Owen stopped fastening the buttons and shook his head. No. I can't let him do that.

Why not? He's your kin...and your boss.

But...I don't really know him. At least that much was true.

Naturally. But it's your special day and he wants it to be that way.

A special day? All Irving Spencer had to do was show up in town and it was a special day? Owen shook his head. Irving must be an important man.

Alright. I have your measurements down, so I'll get started on your other clothes. I'll have them delivered to your new residence by tomorrow afternoon.

My new residence? You mean the sheriff's house?

Ernie threw back his head and laughed. Oh, Irving.

Meyer didn't tell me you had a sense of humor.

Owen watched, bewildered, as the man went into the backroom. He took that as his cue to leave. He quickly dug out a coin that he figured would cover the cost of the suit and threw it on the counter by the cash register. Then he retrieved Irving's hat from the trash can and put it on his head.

So, it didn't match. Who cared? He just had to get out of town before the sheriff realized the truth.

Just as he opened the door, the sheriff stood right in front of him, and he jerked back. He tumbled and fell back against the shirt display which came crashing on top of him as he landed on the floor.

What's going on? Ernie yelled as he came running from the backroom.

The sheriff laughed. Looks like I scared poor Irving. I was ready to come in when he opened the door.

He turned to Owen and stretched his hand out to him. —I guess the groom is anxious to see his bride.

Owen's jaw dropped. What?

The sheriff leaned forward and practically picked Owen up and set him on his feet. He sighed. You can't wear that hat anymore. It doesn't fit you right. Here. He grabbed another hat from the wall, took off the one Owen was wearing, and placed the new one on Owen's head. Much better.

I'll get the shirts on the floor, Ernie told Owen. Go on ahead.

Yep. We don't want to keep that bride of yours waiting.

She's anxious to see you, the sheriff said. Ernie, send me the bill.

Will do.

The sheriff wrapped his arm around Owen's shoulders, forcing Owen out of the store.

Irving's getting married? Owen asked dumbly.

You know, you're a breath of fresh air, son. I can't tell you how nice it is to finally have a deputy who has a sense of humor.

A breath of fresh air? A sense of humor? Owen gulped the lump in his throat as he struggled to keep up with the older man's fast pace on the boardwalk. He caught sight of the train station and wondered if he could create a diversion so he could get there.

I tell you, you had us mighty worried, Meyer continued.

Especially Delia. She's been fretting something awful. I can't tell you how much it means to her that you're doing this.

This? You mean the... Oh goodness. Dare he actually say it? Wedding?

What else?

He glanced at the train as it pulled into the station. Oh, this was bad. Really bad. He had to get out of here! He couldn't marry someone else's woman. He licked his dry lips and cleared his throat.

You know, I...I need to...to... To do what? Think, Owen. Think!

Now, now. Did you think I'd forget?

Owen couldn't answer. He was breathing too fast. Was he hyperventilating? He did feel dizzy, almost like he was going to pass out. He tried to get a gulp of air but coughed instead.

Here it is. The man handed him something. I kept it safe for you, just as you requested.

Owen stared at the wedding band in the palm of his hand. Shaking his head, he said, —You...you don't understand.

Cold feet, huh? Well, all men get that. Even the tough ones.

No. I- He almost tripped on a step as the sheriff led him down the boardwalk so they could cross the dusty street.

Watch your step, son. You don't want to get this nice suit dirty.

Owen gave a frantic look at the train station. This wasn't good. This wasn't good!

The courthouse is right up ahead. Owen dug his heels into the dirt, but the sheriff lifted him by the shoulders and dragged him along, making him stumble a couple of steps before he found his footing and walked with him.

What a joyous day this will be! Now Delia can rest assured that her little boy will be safe.

Little boy? She has a child. —Don't act so surprised. That's why you two are getting married.

It is?

They stopped in front of an imposing building and the older man set his hands on Owen's shoulders. Now, I know you've never been a family man, but you're about to become one.

I feel responsible for you, what with you being so young and all, but I know your ma raised you right. You'll do right by Delia and Johnny.

Johnny. They need you.

Uh...no, I don't think-

Oh, here she comes. She's the one in the pretty white dress. She even sewed it herself.

Owen grabbed the sheriff's vest. You don't understand.

I can't marry her! It was bad enough he stole Irving's clothes and money.

He didn't need to add this to his list of sins.

Meyer chuckled and shook his head. The jokes just never stop with you, do they? Look behind you.

He reluctantly obeyed and straightened as soon as he saw her. Whoa! She was...She was...He rubbed his eyes and looked again just in case they were playing tricks on him. But they weren't. She was the most beautiful woman he'd ever seen.

He blinked several times. She was still there...and looking very appealing.

She had light blond hair that fell softly past her shoulders, a white hat with a red flower on it, a white dress that hung nicely along her curves, and a red floral bouquet in her hand. She smiled at him as she approached him. Two women and two children followed behind her, and a boy stood to her left.

Hello, Irving, she said.

Who? Owen asked.

Meyer waved his hand at her. Oh, don't mind him. This one is a hoot. A real kidder, huh? the blond woman standing on Delia's right said. Well, I'm Delia's sister, Sandy. And this is our sister-in-law, Mary.

Owen couldn't take his eyes off Jenny. He tried to...but he couldn't.

I really appreciate this, Irving.

Delia glanced down at her son and smiled. We both do.

Owen knew he should tell them all the truth. This was the time to do so.

He took one last look at the train station and then turned his attention to Delia. Was there really a contest? She was much more attractive. And Irving wasn't here. And everyone expected Delia to get married today. And Jenny looked very happy about it.

He looked down at the boy. How old are you?

Four, Johnny answered.

You have been taking good care of your ma? he asked.

The boy puffed up his chest and nodded. Yes, sir.

The group chuckled.

Well, the boy seemed like a good kid. Owen returned his gaze to Delia who appeared hopeful. Who was he to let them all down? A big smile crossed his face. Let's get married!

Right this way, the sheriff said, motioning to the courthouse.

Make sure you ask for Judge Johnson, Sally spoke up.

He's my husband, she told Owen.

Owen felt a momentary flicker of panic slither up his spine. He was going to work for the sheriff and his brother-in-law was going to be a judge. Was this a good idea? Maybe he should bolt for the train.

Delia touched his arm. I promise not to overwhelm you with everyone in my family until you get settled into your life here.

Sandy laughed. We are a large bunch, especially when you consider all our children.

That was when Owen noticed the other two boys. Are they yours too? he asked Delia.

No. Greg is Sally's son and Isaac is Mary's son, she said. I did make it clear that I only had one child in my letter, didn't I?

He blinked. A letter? Uh...right. It's been a hectic...uh...journey here. Now that was the understatement of the century!

Well, I was afraid you weren't going to make it, she replied. I'm glad you did.

She had such a nice smile that made her face light up. I am too.

Great, the sheriff said. It looks like you two will be a good match.

Owen couldn't agree more. He knew he'd just met her, but he was already in love with her.

They followed Meyer into the courthouse and requested to see Judge Johnson for the nuptials. The judge agreed to perform the ceremony and it was over before Owen knew what was happening to him.

He experienced that slight twinge of discomfort over being called Irving Spencer during the vows but promised that he'd do good by Delia.

When it came to sign the marriage license, he waited until Delia, the judge, the sheriff, and Sandy signed their names before he reluctantly took the fountain pen.

He glanced at it and frowned. These things leaked when one pressed on the tip just right. His heart raced and he debated how to do this without looking obvious about it.

He leaned over the paper, hoping to block their view and quickly signed his real name, pressing harder into the paper than necessary.

As soon as the ink sprayed over his signature, he took a moment to inspect it. Did it look good enough? Could anyone tell it read Owen Russell instead of Irving Spencer?

The sheriff glanced over his shoulder.

Owen jerked back, his heart hammering loudly in his chest. The sheriff would see it. He'd know for sure. Owen just knew it!

But the sheriff shrugged and said, Those darned pens. Oh well. No matter. The deed is done and handed the license to Owen.

Better take good care of that. Owen stared at him. That was it? He was safe?

The sheriff turned to the judge and started talking as if nothing was wrong.

He quickly tucked the license into his suit pocket. There. No harm done.

The sheriff patted him on the back, startling him. You're a married man now. I know you wrote that nothing is more thrilling than fighting the bandits, but I think you'll find marriage has its own adventures, even if you didn't seem to think so.

Owen glanced over at Delia who stood with Sandy and Mary and their children who doted over her. Irving said that going after bandits was more thrilling than marrying Delia?

Well, the man hadn't seen Delia, so Owen reckoned he'd say that but still... Maybe Irving was a fool. If that was the case, then Delia was better off with a man who preferred her to his job.

Delia's gaze met his and she gave Sandy and Mary a hug before she took Johnny's hand and walked over to him. You must be tired after your long trip here. Would you like to go home and get some rest?

Owen nearly jumped with joy. Going home...with it sounded, that sounded like a good idea.

Stopping himself from dragging her and Johnny out of there, he casually stretched.

Well, I am a little tired. Tired of being around other people, that is.

The sheriff grabbed his arm before he could turn and leave with his new wife and son. Now, I know you have got a honeymoon to enjoy, so I'm giving you three days before you must report to work.

You two also need to check out that house up by the lake I'm giving you. But you must pay me for it with a percentage of your earnings.

A house? Owen glanced at Delia and Johnny. Where were they staying right now? You don't live with your parents, do you? Not that it would have stopped him from enjoying his wedding night, but it wasn't the most comforting feeling to be near her parents when such an event was occurring.

No. I live at the boarding house.

Now you see why it's important that you and your wife and son get a home of your own, Meyer added.

It's a nice out of-the-way place with a good five acres of land. You'll have plenty of privacy and can even get a dog or two for the boy to play with.

A dog? Johnny excitedly asked. Can we get a dog, Ma?

If your pa says it's alright. She looked at him.

Like Owen had the strength to deny her anything. Just looking at her made him weak. Sure, we can get a dog. A boy needs an animal to be friends with.

He bent forward so he was eye level with the boy. When I was a kid, I had a shaggy dog that would chase sticks I threw for it.

He stood up and turned to the sheriff. You said the house is by a lake. How are the fish in that lake?

He shrugged. Fine, I guess.

Well, I can fish. He looked back at the boy. Do you know how to fish?

The boy shook his head.

He glanced over at Delia who was smiling at them. Mind if I teach him?

She chuckled. Of course not. You're his father now. I want you to do things with him.

Sandy walked over to them and nodded. Johnny needs a father. I think you'll do just fine for that, Irving. Welcome to the family.

It took Owen a moment to realize when Sandy said Irving', she meant him.

Oh, right. I'm going to do just that. He shook the judge's hand and then the sheriff's.

Well, Delia, are you ready?

Sure. She waved to everyone.

Don't be a stranger, Sandy called out.

Sandy and her husband began walking. Let them be along for a while.

Oh, it's just an expression, Rick, she retorted, rolling her eyes even as she giggled.

Owen took Delia by the arm and said, we promise to make an appearance occasionally. The group laughed.

He breathed a sigh of relief as he left with Delia and Johnny. Thank goodness that was over.

He'd been right there in front of a judge and lawman and lived through it. Maybe everything was going to be alright after all.

Maybe he could make a life here and be safe. One look at Delia took his mind off the Wanted: Dead or Alive poster. He was now a married man, and married men got to enjoy being in bed with a woman. This was going to be worth all the stress of the past month.

CHAPTER 5

The Boarding House

As soon as Delia closed the door to the room in her boarding house, Owen frowned. Is this it?

She nodded. I know it's small, but it's all Johnny and I needed. Well, until now.

His gaze drifted from the small boy to the two beds. One was his, obviously, and the other was hers, but this wasn't what he expected. He cleared his throat.

Can I talk to you... He glanced at the space that consisted of a dresser and a washstand.

Over there, he finally said, pointing at the window on the other side of the room, which was only a few paces away.

At her prompting, Johnny went over to a box in the corner of the room and pulled out a toy train set.

What is it? she asked, looking concerned. Um... He tried to think of how to phrase this. Lowering his voice so the kid wouldn't overhears, he asked, Is someone going to watch him tonight?

No, she whispered. He stays with me. Yes, but he glanced at Johnny who was focusing on his toy and asked what about us. You know. It is our wedding night.

Her eyes grew wide. Oh. Don't worry about that. I understand. You don't have to feel awkward about it.

Awkward about what?

Your inability to...consummate the marriage.

My inability to what? he shrieked.

Johnny looked over at them.

Delia set her hand on Owen's arm and smiled at her son.

Everything is fine, honey. Keep playing. She turned her attention back to Owen and whispered, you explained that in your letter.

Remember that accident you had?

Accident? he dumbly repeated, unable to believe this horrible thing was happening to him. Here he was, married to a beautiful woman...and he couldn't consummates their marriage?

She walked across the room and pulled out a letter from one of the dresser drawers.

As she made her way back to him, he had a sinking feeling that he wasn't going to be like this.

He reluctantly took the folded piece of paper from her and opened it up. He slowly read the letter, realizing that Irving came off as a very orderly and formal man, so unlike him. His heart sank when he got to the part where Irving made his confession about not being able to perform in bed. Then Owen wondered exactly what kind of accident would render a man unable to make love.

He cringed at the different scenarios that ran through his head. Was Irving stabbed, shot at, or what?

I just want you to know that I will honor our wedding vows, she said. I'm in this for life.

But... He looked back at the letter. Did this mean he couldn't ever...? He glanced back at her, fighting the urge to cry.

This wasn't right. I mean... What could he say that wouldn't give away the fact that he wasn't really Irving? It's just that...

Just that what? He was lying about being Irving so he wouldn't be arrested and hanged? Her brother-in-law was a judge. She'd turn him in!

She smiled. I don't think you're less of a man because of this. To be honest, it's a relief.

His eyes nearly popped out of his head. It is? Shrugging, she took the letter from him. This means we can work on being friends.

I never really was friends with Johnny's father. All he could think about was one thing. At least with you, you'll want to know me. That is, I hope you will.

He felt his heart soften. Of course, I want to know you.

You're my wife.

I'm glad to hear that, Irving. I must admit that I was unsure about this. You sounded nice enough in your letter, but I got the feeling that you wanted to treat our marriage like a business.

Really? No. I don't want that.

I don't either.

Alright. So, he wouldn't get to have fun in bed with her that night. He had to figure out a way to make Irving's problem go away so that he could consummate the marriage, but he realized that she needed to have a husband who was her friend first.

He took her hand and led her to the bed where he sat next to her. He would have picked chairs, but none were in the room.

Why don't you come over here, squirt? he called out to Johnny.

Bring that toy of yours over if you want.

Johnny picked up his train and several tracks and plopped them on the floor right in front of them.

While he assembled the tracks together, Owen turned to Delia. I think there's something we need to discuss before anything else.

He knew this was another lie, but he couldn't give away that he was a man convicted of murder, even if that murder was self-defense. Taking a deep breath, he said, I'd like you to call me Owen.

She furrowed her eyebrows. Why Owen? I'd think your nickname would be something like Irv.

My aunt called me Owen. Because that was his name, but there was no need to tell her all that. But I'd rather you call me Irving in public.

She shrugged. Alright.

Well, that was simple enough. He was surprised, but relieved, she accepted it as easily as she did. So, tell me about you and Johnny here.

He motioned to the boy who seemed focused on his train, though Owen suspected the youngster was paying close attention to everything that was going on.

There's not much to tell really. I already explained about his father. I'm glad that you came. You have no idea how worried I was that you weren't going to show up.

He considered her words and realized that she had written to the real Irving and explained everything to him. That, of course, meant he was supposed to already know about her past...or at least her past with Johnny's father. He couldn't ask her to explain it to him again or else she'd suspect something was up.

So that was a dead end. Clearing his throat, he opted for another avenue. What are you interested in?

Well, I like to sew. That's how I've been supporting me and Johnny.

You sew clothes?

And blankets. I make my own clothes. See?

You made this dress? She wanted to look pretty, Johnny said. Do you like it?

Owen examined the white dress that was simple in its design, but the way it fit on her was what got his attention. It showed off her curves, and he liked that.

It was a shame he wouldn't be able to enjoy those curves if Irving had that stupid impotence problem. He really had to figure a way out of that one. There was no way he could be married to someone as gorgeous as Delia and not enjoy the benefits of marriage.

Owen? Delia asked.

Owen blinked and forced his mind off what she might look like naked. Oh. Yes, I do. I like the dress.

Especially the way you look when you wear it. He had to get his mind onto something else. So, what else do you like to do?

I like to sing.

Really? Are you any good?

She sings like an angel, Johnny spoke up. The preacher says so.

Is that true? Owen looked at her. Will you sing something so I can hear?

She blushed. I don't know...

Oh, come on. It's just us.

Well, I know but... I mean, I don't really know you that well.

That's why we're doing this. To get to know each other.

She looked down at her lap and fiddled with the sleeve on her dress. I don't even know what to sing.

Owen smiled. He thought it was cute that she was shy about singing for him.

Anything will do. What about the Star-spangled Banner by Francis Scott Key?

I like that one, Johnny agreed.

There. If your son wants it, then you should sing it for him.

She shifted on the bed and cleared her throat. Alright.

She licked her lips and straightened her back. She took a deep breath before she began singing.

Owen's mouth almost dropped open. He thought she would have a pleasant voice, but he wasn't prepared for how good she really was. Johnny stopped playing with his toy and watched, probably just as transfixed as he was. The sound of her voice evoked a wave of emotions that surprised him.

When she finished, he struggled to find the right words to express what he thought, but had to settle for a simple, that was beautiful.

She shrugged, her face a bright shade of red. It's the song.

He shook his head and laughed. Granted, the song stirs the spirit, but I've never heard anyone do it the justice you just did.

She peered up at him. Really?

Yes, and I'm not just saying that.

Thank you.

I told you, Ma. You've got the best voice in town.

In town? I'd venture to say she's got the best voice in the country, he told the boy.

I doubt that she said. What about you, Owen? What kind of things do you like to do?

He wondered what Irving told her about him. He decided to feel out the question she just asked so he wouldn't inadvertently say something contrary to what Irving already said.

You know, I'm having trouble remembering what I wrote. I was busy that day when I wrote the letter assuming, of course, that there was only one letter so could you refresh my memory?

Were you locking up the bad men? Johnny asked, his eyes wide.

Yes, he lied.

What did they do? Johnny dropped his toy and sat beside him on the bed.

Uh...bad things. He glanced at Delia who looked at her son in amusement. Realizing the boy wanted to hear something exciting, he continued, they were wanted men. They robbed five banks in three months.

Wow! Did you catch them in a bank?

I did. They came in to rob the place when I was making a deposit.

What's a deposit?

A deposit is when someone puts money into their account.

What's an account?

He paused, wondering how to best explain it to the kid.

The bank holds money for me. So, I took my money into the bank so they could put it into my account...for safe keeping.

Why? Can't you hide it under your mattress like Ma does?

Johnny, Delia interrupted, some people like to keep their money in banks.

She looked at Owen. Go on.

Owen nodded. —Right. There were six of them.

Six? The boy's eyes grew as big as saucers.

They were tall too. I think three of them were seven feet tall.

Seven feet tall? Delia asked, obviously not believing it.

He winked at her, and she grinned. She'd recognize the tall tale for what it was, but a boy had to believe in little guys like Owen taking on men the size of monsters. It made for good daydreams. At least it did for him when he was a kid. He patted Johnny on the shoulder.

I had to be calm through the whole thing. It wasn't easy. They were huge and mean.

Did they have guns?

You bet they did. That's how they were able to talk all those other banks out of their money.

Did you shoot any of them?

No. I did shoot the guns out of their hands, but it took a careful aim to do that. You see when you're outnumbered, you got to use your head and think of how to outwit the bully.

I threw something across the room to distract them and was able to shoot the guns out of their hands, just like that. He snapped his fingers.

You mean you're a quick shot?

Well, I don't want to brag... because he'd never shot a gun in his entire life...but they didn't call me fast fingers for nothing.

Wow.

I then lassoed them all together in one fell swoop and dragged them off to jail.

Not that he'd ever held a lasso before, but he had to finish with something credible. How else would he get six large men rounded up so they didn't run off?

Ma was right about you, Johnny said. You really are the best!

Is that what you said? Owen asked her. Was Irving that great of a deputy?

She nodded. It showed in the way you wrote. I've never seen a man more dedicated to his career.

Oh. Oh boy. Owen exhaled. If Irving had the potential to be that good, then he had a lot to learn about being Irving when he was on duty. He wondered if he could possibly fill Irving's shoes.

CHAPTER 6

The Lie

Owen groaned and rolled over in the bed. Maybe he should sleep on the floor. Lying next to Delia in the dark was driving him insane.

The bed wasn't that big, and the fact that Johnny was asleep in the small bed next to them wasn't that much of a limitation. At least, it wasn't as much of a prevention as it should have been.

He closed his eyes and tried to focus on what he needed to do. Really, he had some serious problems coming up. If Irving had been a fisherman, there wouldn't be anything to worry about.

But Irving wasn't a fisherman. He was a deputy. And apparently, a good one. In fact, from reading Irving's note, Owen could tell that the man took his job seriously.

Owen tried to imagine doing the things that deputies did...whatever those things might be.

Chasing the outlaws, naturally, was one of them. He never thought that he'd be one of those outlaws.

Seeing his face on a Wanted poster had been a chilling experience. Killing Michael had been as well, but that wasn't intentional. The man was coming after him. What else could he do? If he hadn't defended himself, he'd be dead.

Don't think about that. He had to concentrate on being Irving. Irving was brave. Irving was large. How tall was he anyway? A good six feet at least. Maybe six and a half. He recalled how happy Irving had seemed to run into Big Roy and his men.

Owen shivered. Those were scary men, but Irving looked at them in the same way a cat looked at a mouse. Irving, it seemed, enjoyed tracking down outlaws with great enthusiasm.

The man didn't just like his job. He lived for it. It was in his blood. How was Owen supposed to imitate that kind of dedication?

Delia sighed in her sleep and snuggled against his back. He gritted his teeth. This was horrible. She was full of softness and curves. His body insisted he act on the urges coursing through him, but how could he when Irving was impotent? Tears sprang to his eyes.

This wasn't fair. Of all the things the invincible Irving could do, making love to his wife wasn't one of them. She wrapped her arm around his waist. He winced. Was she trying to kill him?

He explored the floor. Was there enough space for him to sleep there? Probably not. The room was way too small. He wondered what was going to happen once they got to the house.

Would he get his own room, or would he be forced to endure this hardship there too? And that brought up another good question.

Just when would they move to the house? They really needed a bigger place, especially with the three of them. He hoped he'd get his own room. No. That's not what he hoped for.

Not really. What he really wanted was for Irving to overcome his problem. He would have to come up for a way to make that happen because he had every intention of doing more than cuddling with his wife.

Owen stopped in front of the jailhouse. Taking a deep breath, he straightened his new vest and wiped imaginary lint from his denims. He did like his new clothes.

The tailor did an excellent job. Alright. Enough stalling. It was time to report to work.

He stood up straight and stared at the door. He could do this. Everything would be fine. All he had to do was follow the sheriff's instructions and things would work out.

He had to believe that because if he didn't, he'd doom himself. The confidence had worked when he got his aunt's money back, and it would work this time. Always think positive.

He opened the door and walked into the jailhouse. Currently, two cells are inhabited. A quick glance around the large room showed him that the sheriff was nowhere in sight. He approached the desk with a pile of papers on it and wiped his sweaty palms when he realized that one of the top pages on the stack was information about him.

There it was in black and white. Owen Russell was last seen heading west on a train. He is 5'8" and has blond hair and a beard. He is wanted for murder.

If you see him, apprehend him, and notify the Baton Rouge, Louisiana marshal.

Owen took the piece of paper and stuffed it into his pocket. He glanced over his shoulder.

One prisoner was asleep and the other had his head bowed in a book. Owen took off his hat and wiped the sweat from his brow. Why was it so hot in Nebraska? He couldn't recall sweating this much in Louisiana.

Then again, he hadn't been on the run when he lived there. He knew it was nerves caused him to break out into a sweat.

The door behind him opened and he whirled around to see the sheriff enter the building. —Good to see you, Irving. You know, you could have asked for more than three days off to be with that bride of yours.

Really? Owen had assumed he'd be expected to show up for work as soon as possible. He mentally kicked himself for that assumption. He'd rather spend the day with Delia and Johnny than be here.

But I shouldn't be surprised. I know that yours is a marriage of convenience.

Lucky me. Owen decided not to voice the sarcastic thought. Instead, he shrugged. So, what are you going to have me do today?

The first thing I need to do is show you your desk. He pointed to the desk against the wall. There it is.

At least I won't get lost on my way to it, he joked.

The sheriff chuckled. I know that the last thing you want to do is sit behind a desk, but I really need you to sort through all this paperwork. Meanwhile, I need to escort Benny over there to the judge.

Owen looked at the man who was reading in his cell.

What did he do? He lowered his voice so Benny wouldn't overhears him.

He got into a brawl at the saloon the other night and shot a man. It wasn't planned or anything.

In fact, some witnesses say that he was defending himself. Owen tuned into everything the man was telling him.

Oh. What will happen to him?

I'm not sure. That's up for the judge to decide. The witnesses are due to show up in court.

Well, you'll let him go, right? I mean, he had to shoot to save his life.

If the judge finds him innocent, then yes. But you see, the issue is proving that he did shoot in self-defense. That's the part that matters.

Right. Of course. Owen rubbed his stomach, hoping to ease the crazy knots it was making. What if no one could prove that he killed Michael in self-defense?

The sheriff patted him on the shoulder.

I'll be back around lunch. Then you can take your break. For the time being, I need you to file all these papers. And don't worry. We'll get you out chasing outlaws soon enough. I know you're eager to get into the action.

That's alright. I don't mind doing this. He much preferred doing this. It was safer than being in the line of duty where men used guns and knives.

Sheriff Meyer unlocked the prisoner's cell and led him to the front door. He stopped and told Owen, try not to let Danny back there bother you. He has a habit of mumbling in his sleep when he's drunk. I see him a lot.

Owen nodded. A regular. He suspected he'd be seeing a lot of Danny in the future. Clearing his throat, he told the man who walked beside the sheriff, good luck.

The sheriff raised an eyebrow at him. The man looked as scared as Owen secretly felt.

Thanks.

Owen could tell the man was innocent just by looking at him. Couldn't Meyer see the same thing?

After they left, he went to the window and watched as they crossed the street. He prayed that the man would be acquitted. If the man was released, then maybe Owen stood a chance as well...should his secret be discovered.

The sleeping man snorted and muttered something about red dancing dots.

Owen shook his head and turned to the desk.

Being drunk made some people say strange things. He sorted through the stack of papers and was relieved when none of them pertained to him. Good. At least he could relax for the time being.

Nice to know that the marriage led to a friendship between them.

Are you ready to meet my family? she asked as she tied Johnny's shoes.

Sure. I'll have Johnny here to keep everyone nice, right?

Johnny nodded. You bet, Pa.

See? Johnny will make sure that no one picks on me.

She grinned at her son. You have a tough job. She glanced at Owen.

Fortunately for you, my brothers are very fond of their nephew, so since he likes you, they will too. She stood up and took a deep breath. Let's go. We'll be going to Sandy's house after church.

If Johnny doesn't leave my side, I'll be just fine. He patted Johnny on the shoulder.

Delia grabbed her shawl.

Here. Let me help you with that. Owen moved over to her and put it around her shoulders.

Her face flushed at the nearness of him. She hadn't expected to feel the fluttery sensation in her stomach. Pushing it aside, she turned to hold Johnny's hand.

Well, here goes nothing.

Owen opened the door and waited for them to leave before he stepped out of the room. I think we're a nice-looking family. Don't you?

I sure do, Pa, Johnny said.

Delia hoped her brothers would approve. Though she knew they couldn't do anything about her marriage, she longed for them to accept her husband. After she made the huge error in judgment with David, it'd be nice to know she could do something right...even if the sheriff had to arrange it for her.

On their way to church, Owen slipped his hand through hers. The contact felt natural, as if they had always known each other. It was a wonderful feeling, knowing she was safe with him. He wouldn't run off on her or Johnny.

Somehow, she knew that this was the kind of man she could trust. When they reached the yard, Sandy waved to the other family members. Oh good! Irving's right over there.

Owen must have noticed Delia's anxiety, for he squeezed her hand. Everything's going to be just fine. Then he let go of her and picked Johnny up and told the boy, Now you make sure to tell them lots of good things about me, alright?

I sure will, Johnny assured him, looking unusually serious about his new mission.

Sandy ran up to them with Tom, Jessica, and their girls. This is Irving Spencer, she told them. He's Sheriff Meyer's new deputy. Irving, this is our brother Tom and his wife Jessica and their pretty little girls. She turned to Owen. Did you bring your badge?

No, Owen replied. I only wear it when I'm on the job. Oh. That's a shame.

It sure is, the oldest girl agreed. I've never seen a deputy badge before.

I'll have to grab it before I head on out to your grandparents' farm for the family get-together, Owen promised.

Can I try it on?

Sure.

Why would you want to do that? Tom asked. You won't be a deputy.

It's just for fun, Jessica said. I think it's a great idea. Tom shook his head. You won't let them climb trees because you say they're acting like boys, but you'll let them wear a badge?

They won't fall and break a limb if they put on a badge. They could get stuck with the pin. Those things are sharp.

She rolled her eyes. You manage just fine around sharp objects, and they will too.

I managed to help build our new house, didn't I? I stood high up on the roof for that one. That means the girls can climb trees without breaking a bone.

Yes! The girl jumped up and down with her two sisters. It's true. We saw Pa up there. He even hopped on one foot.

Delia gasped. You did that on the roof?

To make sure I wouldn't fall through it.

She shook her head in disbelief. I hate to think what chances you take when I'm not looking.

I'm fine. The girls are fine. Everyone's fine.

Sandy groaned. That's enough. This is about Irving, not girls climbing trees. She scanned the yard. I'll get David and Mary. They usually get people to stop arguing.

As she ran off, Delia wrinkled her eyebrows and looked at Tom. What is wrong with your sister? Why does she think we're arguing?

He shrugged. Who knows? Sandy tends to go overboard on things to meet you, Irving. I see that Johnny that you do, Delia replied.

Owen chuckled before looking between Jenny and Tom.

I can tell you're related. You look a lot alike. Oh really? Tom's eyebrows rose in a challenge. Can you tell where the other siblings are in this crowd?

Delia watched in amusement as Johnny leaned forward to whisper in Owen's ear. She nudged her son in the side. There'll be no cheating. He must figure this one out on his own.

That's right, Owen agreed. It wouldn't be fair to make this easy for me.

Johnny looked disappointed but kept quiet.

After a full minute of inspecting everyone assembled on the lawn, he finally pointed out Richard, Joel, and Dave. Well, that brother over there is pretty much a given since Sandy is leading him over here.

Tom and Jessica's girls watched Owen in obvious shock.

You're amazing, one of them said.

No wonder you're a good deputy. You can probably figure out who's an outlaw just by looking at them, the other added.

Owen shrugged. It's nothing. Really. I mean, the Larsons all have the same shade of blond hair and cheekbones and chin. It was easy.

Not all of us can do that, Jessica said.

Sandy came up to them, holding a one-year-old boy in her arms. This little man here is Isaac.

Same blond hair as the others, Owen told Delia.

Notice the same streaks of white, blond through the golden layers?

Delia inspected the hair and then took in Tom's hair and Dave's hair. By golly if her new husband wasn't right. Even a look at Johnny showed the same trait. It was uncanny that a man could detect subtle details like that.

Sandy turned to the couple next to her. This is Isaac's pa, David. And there's his ma, Mary. They were made for each other.

Delia blinked and took a good look at her older sister. Was there a hint of sorrow in Sandy's voice?

Before she could further contemplate what was going on with her sister, Isaac threw his arms around Sandy's neck and kissed her cheek. Sally laughed. I'm his favorite aunt.

I beg your pardon. Delia glanced at Amanda as she and Richard walked up to them.

Sandy turned to Amanda. Well, it's true. I'm the favorite. Don't you all agree? she asked the children.

Delia's parents hustled over to them. Oh good, her father said. I finally got to meet my new son-in-law.

Delia smiled sympathetically at Owen as he shook her father's hand. Her poor husband was being surrounded by a group of strangers. He glanced at her way, and she gave a slight shrug.

To her surprise, he winked at her. I think I can handle it. After all, I got Johnny to help me remember names. You'll do that for me, right?

JOhnny nodded. I will.

Delia had to admit that Owen could handle the onslaught of her family with amazing ease. She guessed that was part of what made him a good deputy. He didn't crack easily under pressure and he must have felt some kind of pressure.

Her family inspected him with open curiosity. She finally decided that being a part of the Larson family was not for the faint of heart.

The church bell rang, announcing that service would soon begin. As the group dissipated to assemble into the building, Owen placed his arm around her shoulders and drew her close.

That wasn't so painful, was it?

Startled, she blinked. Painful?

You looked like you were ready to flee, he said.

Did I?

Johnny leaned forward. Ma hates large gatherings. She blushed and cleared her throat. It was true. Even if it was her family, she preferred there to be less of them bunched around her at the same time.

Owen kissed her cheek.

Her skin tingled with warmth from the simple contact.

It's alright. You can lean on me if you get overwhelmed in the future. Now, we better get in there before they start the hymns, he said.

Once again, he took her hand, and her heart gave a tiny flutter. It'd never been this nice with David. You're nothing like I thought you'd be.

I hope that's a good thing.

She smiled. It is. Then she turned her attention to the Church.

CHAPTER 7

The House

Delia couldn't hide her excitement as she took Johnny to the house. They'd be moving into a house. One that would have a kitchen, a parlor, and a couple of bedrooms. There would also be land for Johnny to run around on. She couldn't wait!

It would be wonderful to get out of the boarding house. As nice as her landlady was, Delia longed for a place to call her own.

Now she could make breakfast for her husband and son, see her husband off to work, and watch Johnny run around outside.

Owen agreed that they could get a dog, so Johnny would finally have the pet he always wanted.

As she walked with Johnny down the boardwalk, Johnny said, I really like Pa. Do you like Pa?

She smiled. Yes. I do. Owen was turning out to be a lot of fun. From his formal letter, she'd never guess he had the kind of personality that naturally drew people to him.

Already, her brothers liked him and they weren't easy to please.

He's going to take me fishing. Are we going to live by a lake?

That's what the sheriff said. She didn't know who was more excited about fishing: Owen or Johnny.

We're a real family now, aren't we?

She stopped and looked at him. He'd always wanted a father, one who was there for him. Yes. We are.

Am I going to have brothers and sisters?

She didn't know why the question should make her blush, but it did. No, honey.

Why not?

There was no way she could tell her son about Owen's problem, so she opted for a little white lie. Well, it's not meant to be.

Oh. I will pray for one.

Uh... She didn't know what to say to that. The boy could pray all he wanted, but there were some things that just weren't going to happen. Finally, she settled for shrugging her shoulders.

Alright. Let the boy pray. He'd figured it out when he was an adult and still the only child.

They turned their attention back to the boardwalk and stopped in front of the mercantile in time for David to approach them. She instinctively placed her hands on her son's shoulders.

David smiled at Johnny. Hi there, Johnny. Do you remember me?

Johnny looked hesitant.

What are you doing, David? she demanded, her hands tightening on her son's shoulders.

Ow, Johnny said.

She relaxed her fingers. Sorry, honey.

David handed Johnny a coin. Why don't you go in there and buy a piece of candy. I want to talk to your ma.

She bit back a protest. He had no right to give her child anything, but she knew that if Johnny didn't go into the store, then David would talk to her with him right there. She had no intention of getting him involved in this mess if she could avoid it.

Once Jeremy ran into the store, David frowned at her.

She braced herself. Here it came.

I see you got married, he sourly stated.

Really? I don't recall you being there when it happened.

He grunted. Hmm... Funny. I should be amused. Who knew you had a sense of humor.

Why can't you just scurry on out of here like you did when you found out I was expecting Johnny?

Oh, honey. I'm not going anywhere. I meant what I told our boy in there.

He nodded in Johnny's direction. That fancy new husband of yours may be married to you, but he's not Johnny's father.

He is according to the law. I've got full rights to my son.

You won't be taking him away from me.

He's got my blood in him, and there's no court of law that's going to change that. I will be a part of his life, whether you're married or not.

No! Her heartbeat accelerated. You need to get out of here.

I will not.

He didn't even look like he cared that he was upsetting her, and that only served to upset her more. He enjoyed this. She just knew he did! Why are you doing this to me?

I'm not doing anything to you. You may be married to that deputy, but Jeremy will always be my boy.

She glared at him. She couldn't believe this was the same man who, just five years ago, had been sweet and kind. And she had been such a fool to not listen to her parents.

They had warned her to wait until she was married, but she thought she knew better and just look at where that got her! She glanced at Johnny who paid for the piece of candy and plopped it into his mouth. Her son was the only good thing that came out of her time with David. Her son. Johnny was hers. Not David's.

A man who ran off to avoid taking responsibility for his actions was not a father, and no he has my blood argument would change that.

Her gaze met David's in a challenge. You'll have to get through my husband. You've heard of his reputation, I'm sure.

He's Irving Spencer and he's known for performing great feats on the job. Why, it wasn't too long ago that he single-handedly caught six bank robbers in one fell swoop, and three of them were seven feet tall.

David threw back his head and laughed. I've seen your husband, and he's pathetic. I'm at least six inches taller than him.

Yes, but you're not seven feet tall, which means you're easy bait.

He rolled his eyes.

Finally feeling as if she'd just won the upper hand, she casually shrugged. It doesn't matter what you think. Sheriff Meyer said he's the best, and you know that Meyer isn't one to lie.

Now, if you'll excuse me, I have some things I need to buy. She pushed past him and entered the store. It wasn't until she noticed that he hadn't followed her in that she finally breathed a sigh of relief.

Get me, boy! Sheriff Meyer called out. Sweat ran down Owen's forehead as he pursued the man who was hightailing it down the street with the bag of cash.

Blood pumped through his body with an overwhelming surge of panic. He never should have bragged about catching bank robbers to Johnny because now God saw it fit to show him exactly what dealing with a robber was like and Owen decided that he didn't like it.

Nope. He didn't like it one single bit. The man was fast on his feet, which was surprising when one considered that he was only 5'4. The man was short, but boy, he sure could run. The man glanced over his shoulder and scowled at Owen. Alright. So, the man was also a mean looking fellow.

As much as Owen hated to admit it, this robber intimidated him. But Owen knew he couldn't give into his fears.

He was supposed to be the mighty and brave Irving Spencer who was nothing short of legendary in this town. So, he had to act like he was Irving. And that was proving to be no small feat!

Owen rounded the corner after the legendary bandit as they passed multiple shops along the boardwalk. Along the way, he caught sight of a fishing pole. Inspired, he dug into his pocket, pulled out a coin and flipped it in the store owner's direction as he snatched the pole from the doorway.

He might not be able to run the man down, but he could fish him out of the crowd. He threw back the rod and released the hook.

As he hoped, the hook lodged itself right into the back of the man's shirt and Owen pulled back on it. The man grunted and fell to the ground. Owen then proceeded to reel the robber until he was at Owen's feet.

Wow! a twelve-year-old boy said as he approached Owen. That was amazing!

Out of breath, but grateful the desperate trick had worked, Owen grinned at the boy. Thanks.

How did you flip that rod back like that? It's nothing. I just use my wrist like this. He demonstrated by showing the boy how he angled his wrist. Then I snap it forward in a quick motion.

Just wait until I show that to Cal! Next time we go fishing, we're bound to get the hook far out. Why, that man was a good distance from you. I don't know if you would have caught in any other way.

Sadly, the boy spoke the truth, so Owen didn't deny it. He glanced at his gun in the holster. Maybe instead of the Colt .45, he needed to lug a fishing rod around.

So, you're the new deputy? Irving Spencer?

That's what the sheriff calls me. There. That wasn't a direct lie. What's your name?

Amos.

I'll tell you what, Amos. I already have a couple of fishing rods at home. Would you mind taking this one off my hands?

Honest to goodness?

Yep.

Sure, Mister!

Owen quickly released the hook from the man's shirt and cuffed him before he could get away. Straightening up, he handed the boy the fishing rod. Remember, if you see any bandits running through town, you can be my assistant and catch them for me. But practice on getting those fish first.

The boy's face glowed. I sure will. You can count on me. Owen chuckled. Good.

The sheriff caught up to them and slapped Owen on the back. Well, I'll be. You got them.

He was amazing! the boy exclaimed. I better get to Ma before she starts hollering for me.

As the boy ran off, the sheriff shook his head. I finally got to see Irving in action, and what a sight that was. Did you know I've been trying to get old Joe McGuffy for over two years now. I didn't think that was ever going to happen, but thanks to you, it did.

Really? Owen asked, suddenly feeling better about resorting to using a fishing pole.

That Joe there is the fastest runner around. I've never been able to catch him. The sheriff leaned down and pulled Joe to his feet. Justice will finally be served, and all thanks to my new deputy.

Owen's smile widened. Maybe he wasn't so bad at this job after all.

News of Owen's deed spread fast and within two hours, Delia heard it from Mrs. Diaz who paid her for the two dresses she made for the woman.

He caught fast as a bullet Joe'? Delia asked.

Mrs. Diaz smiled as she held the clothes in her arms.

He sure did. That new husband of yours is a real catch if I ever did hear of one. You did good on this one.

Delia grinned. It was nice to have the respect of being married to a good man. I didn't realize how good I was going to have it when Sheriff Meyer suggested the arranged marriage to me. But it really has worked out.

I'm glad. It's about time you got a good one after that Clyde ran off.

Yes, well, I should have said no.

And what can you do about the past? Nothing. Which is why there's no sense in dwelling on it.

Delia sighed. She feared that she didn't deserve Irving.

When she thought it was just going to be convenient arrangement, it was easier to accept. But Irving was turning out to be a friend too, and there was that part of her that was attracted to him.

He wasn't drop dead gorgeous. He was good looking, but he was more adorable than anything else. Still, he did have a smile that made her heart skip a beat.

Mrs. Diaz giggled and patted her arm. Enjoy the honeymoon. It's the best time in a woman's life.

Delia blushed and said good-bye before she went to Sandy's house to get Johnny. She pulled the shawl around her shoulders, realizing that soon she'd be wearing a coat, and knocked on her sister's front door.

Sandy answered it and waved her in. Did you hear about Irving catching that robber?

I did. News had reached Sandy too. She wondered who didn't know.

He's earning his reputation. Will you stay for a cup of coffee before you head back home?

Remembering that she wanted to talk to Sandy, she nodded.

Are the boys out back?

Yes. Johnny wanted to play with the dog.

Well, we'll get one as soon as we move into the little house the sheriff is selling us. Then your poor dog can get a break.

As they entered the kitchen, Delia took off her shawl while Sandy grabbed two cups from a shelf. Oh please. Johnny is doing Clifford a favor. Greg would rather read.

Delia glanced out the window where the two boys were rolling around in the grass with the dog. Doesn't Greg ever play with him?

Occasionally. But he finds Clifford more interesting when Johnny's interested in him. You know how it works.

Things are more entertaining when someone else takes note of them.

True. She sat down as Sandy poured coffee into the cups.

Once Sandy handed her the cup and sat across from her, Delia said, I noticed you seemed unusually sad on Sunday when you said Dave and Mary were meant for each other.

Sandy groaned. You know me too well.

That's because I'm your sister and I love you.

I know.

So, do you want to tell me what's going on?

Nothing. And that's the problem.

Delia frowned. How could nothing be a problem?

Sandy took a sip of coffee, put the cup on the table and sighed. Rick and I... Well... We're not as close as we once were.

Are you having marital problems?

No. Not really. I mean, we don't argue. It's just that we have a routine, and that routine doesn't allow for much time to be together. You know what I mean?

The romance is gone from your marriage?

Yes. It's like we just got too comfortable with each other, and when I talk to him about it, he says that it means we've been married for nine years and that's normal.

In fact, I can't remember the last time we were intimate. I think it's been five months.

Really? Delia didn't hide her shock.

Rick spends a lot of time studying the law books, and when he gets to bed, he's tired. At least, that's what he says.

She reached out and touched her sister's arm. You think it's another reason?

She shrugged. I wonder if he still likes what he sees when he looks at me. I'm not the young girl he married.

You're still attractive.

I don't feel attractive. Do you know that I got my hair done and even bought a new dress, but he didn't even notice it.

He just came home, gave me the obligatory kiss, and went to read the paper. The paper is more interesting than I am!

Delia grinned. Since when do men notice things like how our hair looks or what we're wearing?

It's not just that. We've been unable to have a conversation that doesn't revolve around Greg. If it weren't for our son, I don't know what we'd talk about.

We're getting old, boring married couple, and I don't want that. I miss how things were when we were first married. Everything was fun and exciting.

I don't think things are supposed to stay that way.

Oh, I realize that. I mean, I know it's not that way all the time. But there should be moments where the spark comes back.

Delia couldn't blame Sandy. It seemed logical.

Enjoy the honeymoon period. Sure, you'll have fights, but there's nothing like that first year you're with your husband.

She smiled wryly. It's not like I have a typical marriage.

Maybe it didn't start that way, but you two look happy together.

I do like Irving. I thought he'd be old and boring, but he's not. However, Delia hesitated to broach a subject that was sensitive, but she thought it might help Sandy feel better about her situation. Well, Irving had an accident back when he lived in South Carolina, and it rendered him unable to perform in bed.

Sandy brought her hand up to her cheek. Oh no!

He wrote to me about it ahead of time, so I knew. I didn't care because I wanted to get married so David would leave me alone, and by the way Irving sounded in the letter, I didn't get the impression that he was likable enough to want to share a bed with.

After dealing with David, I learned the value of a man who was a friend. You know?

Sandy nodded. Of course, I do. No woman wants to be with a man like that if he doesn't truly love her.

Right. And that letter didn't give me any reason to hope that I might be marrying someone who had the capacity to love me. In fact, he seemed much too devoted to his job. In a way, he was already married, and he agreed to marry me to do the sheriff a favor.

So, it's turned out better than you hoped?

Yes, it has, which is why it's a real shame that he can't...you know.

Sandy nodded. I do. At least your husband has a valid reason.

Well, I think it's time that you and Rick got the spark back into your marriage.

Don't think I haven't tried.

Now you have my help. Delia squeezed her sister's hand.

We'll see what we can do about Rick. I know he loves you. He just needs to remember how desirable you are.

From your mouth to God's ears. We'll figure something out, Delia promised.

CHAPTER 8

Overjoy

That Saturday, Owen purchased a wagon and led his new family out to the home that Sheriff Meyer had given them to buy.

The charming little home was situated on the outskirts of town with a good five acres around it and a good-sized lake not too far away. Owen liked it immediately, and he turned to Delia and Johnny who sat beside him in the wagon to see what they thought.

Johnny bounced up and down in between him and Delia.

Wow! This is for us?

It sure is, Owen said. And I'm going to pay for all of it too. It might take a few years, but this is going to be ours.

Then he lifted his gaze to Delia who had the most beautiful smile he'd ever seen on a woman.

What do you think?

She looked at him with tears in her eyes. It's the most wonderful place I've ever seen.

Then there's no need to cry, he teased. Grandpa says women cry over everything; Johnny whispered in his ear.

Don't worry about Ma. That's her happy crying.

He grinned and winked at the boy.

Thanks.

Behind them, a puppy poked Johnny in the back. He picked the dog up and cuddled him the best he could despite the animal's squirming.

That poor thing is more slippery than a fish, Owen said, chuckling as the dog bounded out of the boy's arms and into the back where all their belongings waited for them to take into their new home. He pulled the wagon up to the front door.

There's the barn! He pointed toward the rear of the house.

This place has everything we need, doesn't it?

It sure does!

As soon as the wagon stopped, Johnny crawled over him and climbed down. He turned and caught the anxious puppy.

Rover likes it too!

Well, don't run off too far, Delia called out as the boy and dog headed out to play in the fields.

I won't! he called out, not bothering to look back.

He's a great kid, Owen said. You did a good job raising him.

She shrugged. I did the best I could.

You're not used to taking compliments, are you?

Before she could respond, for he could tell that the question startled her, He wrapped his arm around her shoulders and drew her close.

You're a good woman, Delia. A man couldn't do better than you.

Then, so she wouldn't have to respond for it seemed to him that she'd long ago learned to suppress her vulnerable side, he kissed the top of her head and added, Let's go see if this place is as good inside as it is out.

Blushing, she nodded.

He jumped down and helped her down. She felt good in his arms, so he took a moment to hold her. He wished he could kiss her on the lips, but he wondered if Irving would do that.

What did a man who was unable to consummate a marriage do anyway?

Deciding to press his luck or Irving's luck, he kissed her cheek. She didn't turn away.

In fact, he thought she leaned into him. He knew that was all he could get away with today, so he didn't go any further.

The fact that she allowed him to get close to her lips was enough for the time being. Somehow, he hoped to work his way up to kissing her on the mouth. Then, perhaps, Irving could overcome his problem because she healed him.

Yes, that seemed like a good plan.

Standing up straight, he smiled at her and happily noted she smiled back. You're the prettiest woman I've ever seen. She lowered her eyes and shrugged.

I mean it, Delia. You really are. He took her hand and led her to the front door. After he opened it, he glanced slyly at her.

On impulse, he picked her up.

What are you doing? she asked, surprised.

Carrying my bride over the threshold.

She giggled as he stepped forward.

Oh Owen, what a silly thing to do. But it was very sweet.

Well, I figure this will get us off to a good start on our life together in this house. He gently set her down.

What do you think?

She took her eyes off him and turned to the cozy kitchen. Gasping, she ran to the window.

It has a view of the land! I think I can see the lake from here.

He grinned at her enthusiasm. Every woman needed to have a good view when she cooked a meal, his aunt had often told him.

I hope this will make your hours slaving away in here worth it, he joked.

She looked at him and laughed. I love it. I really do.

I've always wanted a kitchen where I could make meals for my husband and children.

She paused, her face growing red. I mean, of course, you and Johnny. I had this thought long ago when I was a child...

Avoiding eye contact, she turned to inspect the shelves along the wall.

There could be children, Owen thought. As soon as Irving could make that possible... He'd caught the wistful look in her eyes. He suspected that she dreamt of having a house full of children running around and causing chaos everywhere they went.

She did, after all, come from a good-sized family. He rather fancied the notion himself. We'll see, Delia. In due time, our dream might come true.

She inspected the pump at the sink before she touched the round table and four chairs.

The furniture is in good shape.

Curious, he made his way to the parlor and saw the couch and two chairs and table. It looks good here as well. Want to go upstairs and check on the bedrooms?

Our own bedrooms! she squealed as she rushed past him and up the staircase.

He frowned. Our own bedrooms? What exactly did that mean?

She reached the first bedroom and motioned to him.

Come on!

What? Did she find the one he'd be staying in? Was she planning where he would sleep and where she would sleep? Even if he didn't get much sleep next to her in bed, he still wanted to be with her. He'd gotten used to her soft body pressing up against his. Sure, it drove him crazy. But still...the impotence ordeal was temporary.

Owen?

Reluctant, he trudged up the steps. When he reached the bedroom, he saw the small, empty room.

I think Johnny will like this one. It looks out toward the lake. You know, he's excited to learn how to fish. I think looking out his bedroom window will be exciting for him.

Yes.

She took his hand and hurried out of the room, practically dragging him along. She stopped and glanced at the second room which seemed to be the same size as the one she'd just reserved for Johnny.

Maybe we can put the toys in there.

Owen's ears perked up. Toys? As in, this would not be his bedroom? When they reached the last one on the other side of the hallway, he noted it was the largest of the three, and it even came with a bed meant for more than one person.

I love it! She released his hand. Two windows! You can see to the west and the south. Just look at all the land around us. It feels as if we're in our own little world, doesn't it?

My parents bought a house out on a farm because they hated living in the city, so I got used to being out with the fields. I loved it then, and I love it even more now because this is our home.

Right. And this is our bedroom, he said, just to make sure he hadn't misunderstood her intentions.

Yes. Isn't it beautiful? I can't wait to see how my pillows look on the bed. And curtains! Will flowers on curtains bother you if I make them blue?

Relieved that they would still be sharing a bed, he waved his hand and said, Honey, you can have pink flowers for all I care.

You mean it?

Sure.

Well, since you're sincere, I would like pink roses on the curtains. They'd match my pillows and blanket. I never could make those kinds of curtains at the boarding house because it wasn't my place to decorate.

This is your home. Do whatever you want. I'm easy to please.

Feeling like a huge weight had been lifted off his shoulders, he clapped his hands together.

Well, I'm going to start bringing our things in.

She seemed to be so focused on checking the width of the window frame that he didn't bother repeating himself.

He enjoyed seeing her happy, and she was happy. As was he. He wondered how soon was too soon to really get enjoyment out of that bed.

Sandy took a deep breath and examined the new bookcase in the den. She had dusted all the books and placed them on the shelves, just as Rick had arranged them.

He'd been eyeing this bookshelf for a good six months but hadn't bothered to buy it, so she saved up some of their money and thought today might be a good day to give it to him.

The front door opened, and she nearly jumped with delight. Rick was home! She ran to the front door to greet him.

How was your day? she asked.

He looked at her and smiled as he shut the door. It was good. Where's Greg?

He's spending the night at Richard and Amanda's. I thought it'd be nice to have some time to ourselves.

His smile widened and he drew her into his arms.

I can't remember the last time we were alone. What's the special occasion?

Shrugging, she wrapped her arms around his neck. I don't know. I thought it might be nice to be together, just the two of us.

He bent his head and kissed her. Her heartbeat with excitement. She really should have thought of this sooner. Maybe that was why he hadn't been this romantic with her for the longest time. When the kiss ended, she sighed. That was nice.

Nice?

Wonderfully so. Then she remembered his gift. Pulling away from him, she said, I got you something today. Did you? What is it?

He put his hat and light coat on a hook in the closet. You must come with me to find out.

His eyebrows rose in interest. Well, now you got my interest.

She pretended to mope. You mean I didn't have it when I was kissing you?

Chuckling, he tucked his hand around her arm. You already know the answer to that.

Maybe. But it would be nice to hear it. Pushing the matter aside, since it was a minor one, she led him to the den.

Do you notice anything different?

Oh, come on, Sandy. You know I'm no good at these games.

But you'll like this one. Give it a try. Take a good look around and see if there's anything here that you've been wanting for months now.

Alright. He let go of her arm and stood in the middle of the room. After half a minute, he snapped his fingers.

The bookcase?

She nodded. I saved up some extra money and got it today. It looks terrific, doesn't it? I just love oak!

It does look nice.

And I took care to keep your books in the same place where they were on that old bookcase.

He examined the shelves. I see that. He glanced at her.

Thank you, Sandy.

I'm glad you like it.

In fact, this turned out even better than she hoped.

He walked over to her and kissed her.

She leaned into him and let their kiss deepen. Two kisses before supper? She was on a roll, and she planned to do whatever she could keep it going.

He gave a low groan as she wiggled up against him. His hands roamed places they hadn't touched in a while.

Her heart pounded with excitement.

It'd been so long since they made love, but she was ready for it.

A knock at the door interrupted them and he sighed.

Duty calls.

She blinked. Duty? What duty?

He cleared his throat and adjusted his pants. Jack's bringing over the notes for the case I must hear on Monday.

Another hearing?

Judge Townsend got ill, so I'm taking his place.

Again?

The doctor's not sure what's wrong with him. Hopefully, it's something that can be quickly resolved. I hate to think it's something serious.

She followed him out of the room and down the hallway.

But you don't have to start on the notes now. You just got back from visiting the sheriff about the bank robber.

I must study up on this one.

Now?

I'm afraid so.

Her face grew warm with anger as he opened the front door.

Good afternoon, Jack. You got Judge Townsend's notes for me?

Yep. Jack handed over the large stack of papers. Says it's his life's work.

We'll see if we can put this one to rest for his sake then.

Tell him we're praying for him to get better. Will do.

Sandy clenched her teeth and shut the door since Rick's arms were full of work. Work.

That's what she was competing with. It didn't dawn on her until that moment what she was up against.

Rick loved his job. And she was more interesting than his job, wasn't she?

Forcing aside her irritation, she strode after him as he went back to the den.

You know, she sweetly began, it's always a good idea to take a break sometimes. Even I can't go on with the housework and budget unless I take a break.

I know but I need to refresh my memory on this.

He motioned to the papers. That's not the only thing you need to refresh your memory on. Her eyes grew wide. Did she say that aloud?

He placed the ton of papers on his desk and frowned.

What is that supposed to mean?

Well, if the cat was out of the bag... I just think it's been too long since we've been together. You know, as man and wife.

He groaned. I can't. As it is, I'll be up until midnight studying all of this.

But it doesn't take a long time to do what I have in mind.

There's a lot of other things that come into play when we get together.

She crossed her arms, knowing she wasn't going to like this but unable to stop herself from asking the question anyway.

What is that supposed to mean?

It means that you want to talk and cuddle. That will end up taking a couple of hours.

You didn't mind spending a couple of hours with me when we were first married.

Well, I can't spare a couple of hours this weekend.

When can you spare a couple of hours?

I don't know. Townsend might be gone this week.

So, I must wait for whenever you have time to be with me?

He sighed. Don't do this.

Do what? she snapped.

Make this about the way I feel about you. I love you. I never stopped loving you. But I have responsibilities to take care of.

Those responsibilities have nothing to do with me?

Of course, they do. If I didn't work, we wouldn't have a roof over our heads or food to eat.

Then, as if the matter was settled, he sat behind his desk and started sorting through the stack in front of him.

A responsibility? That's all she was to him? Fine, she finally said when her shock wore off. Since you're so busy, I suppose you won't have time to eat supper either!

Before he could protest, she left the room and slammed the door behind her.

CHAPTER 9

Owen at work

Two weeks later, Owen chased the man who just stole another man's horse. The two rode on horseback toward the outskirts of town.

Get back here! Owen yelled.

The thief ignored him.

He groaned. Why couldn't any of the bandits he'd been chasing around actually stop?

He'd love it if one would obey him.

After all, he was the deputy. Shouldn't that carry some weight in this town?

He reached for his fishing rod. Yes, real deputies like Irving Spencer carried a Colt .45. Owen carried a fishing rod. But the rod worked.

He threw back the rod and released the line. It caught onto the belt loop of the man's pants. Even as Owen pulled the rod toward him, he realized that he was falling off his steed.

He struggled to compensate with his weight, but it was no use. He tumbled off the animal and fell right onto the prairie grass.

Still holding onto the rod, he was pulled along the land, being scraped and bruised in places he didn't even know existed.

He screamed and grunted. Where was Sheriff Meyer?

Suddenly, the man stopped his horse.

Owen continued to roll a few turns until he stopped, flat on his back and staring up at the sky. He gasped for air and tried to focus on the clouds. His head was spinning.

To his surprise, the thief walked over to him and handed him the hook.

Whatever did you do something stupid like that for?

Stupid like what?

Like not letting go of that fishing rod. You could have killed yourself.

It didn't occur to me to let go. A fisherman always holds his fishing rod so the fish doesn't get away.

The man laughed and slapped him on the shoulder.

You're the strangest deputy I've ever come across. But I heard that you are an expert with the rod, and darned if that ain't the truth.

Why, you got me good. It took all my strength to hold onto that horse.

Owen grinned at the compliment.

I spent years perfecting the technique.

Well, I hate to see you go through all that trouble to lose, so, I'll tell you what.

You talk that sheriff of yours into going easy on me you know, avoiding that rope and I'll turn myself in.

Really? Was it going to be that easy?

Sure. Why not? You remind me of my brother.

Oh. Just as Owen was about to thank him, he continued, not too bright and clumsy but he's got a good heart.

Owen blinked and gave the man a startled look. Was that a compliment or a put down?

The sheriff called out to them as he rode in their direction.

Don't worry. I got this covered.

The man slapped him on the shoulder again and stood up. I give up. Your deputy got me.

He held up his hands and waited for the sheriff to arrive.

Sighing, Owen stood up. He's returning the horse to its owner. What happens with someone in a case like that?

The sheriff rubbed his chin. I suppose a few nights in jail might be enough since I haven't seen you on any wanted posters.

Wanted posters? Are those serious? Owen asked, hoping he didn't sound too stupid...or guilty.

Of course, they are. Only the worst of the worst get on those.

Oh great. Just what Owen wanted to hear. He could only hope that no more posters of him were being printed and sent out across the state.

Because if the sheriff got a hold of one and Delia saw it... Well, he didn't even want to think of the implication of those events, and hopefully, he never would.

Delia sat next to Sandy who'd stopped by her new home to check it out.

While Johnny played outside with the dog, she faced her sister who looked torn between screaming and crying.

Rick spent the entire weekend locked up in his den. He loves his job more than he loves me.

Delia wished she had some words of comfort to offer her sister, but she couldn't think of anything.

He did kiss you though, and you said it was a good kiss?

I thought so. At least it got me excited. I really thought something interesting was going to happen. But no. Someone came to the door and ruined everything.

Inspiration struck her. I know what you two need! You need time to get away from it all, even if it's a romantic dinner for two. I've tried.

But you didn't get out of the house. Why don't you bring him here? You two can have a nice, relaxing meal.

Take a stroll down the lake or sit on that lovely porch swing. Then Owen and I will watch Greg, and you two can go home alone.

By the time you get back, it'll be too late for anyone to bother you.

Sandy bit her lower lip, as if she considered it. It might work.

It very well might! Why not give it a try? What's the worst that can happen.

He'll talk about his job through the whole meal.

When Delia laughed, she shook her head. Believe it or not, he's done it before.

He even put Greg to sleep one time. The poor child fell forward, and his head landed right in the mashed potatoes.

Well, we'll have to make sure that doesn't happen again.

How? I don't know, but we'll think of something.

The front door opened, and Owen entered the house.

Good afternoon, Sandy. It's good to see you.

What are you doing home so early? Delia wondered.

Sheriff said he had nothing for me to do so I should spend time with my bride.

Sandy gave a wistful sigh. Glancing at Delia, she Whispered.

You're lucky. Turning back to Owen, she smiled and stood.

It's time for me to go anyway. I need to be home when Greg comes back from school.

I finally got to entertain in my own home, Delia told Owen. Then she hugged her sister.

Thanks for coming.

Of course, I came. I had to see why you were so excited about this place.

She stepped to the door which Owen held open for her. There's no need to walk me to the buggy.

After she waved to them, he softly shut the door. You have a great family.

Yes. I know.

Where's Johnny? he asked.

He and the dog are by that big oak tree out front. He said he needed to practice fishing. She chuckled.

He even broke off a thin branch from that tree to use as a fishing rod, and he's pretending the grass is a big lake.

I'll have to go out there with real rods.

Touched, she walked up to him until they were inches apart from each other. You're really going to teach him how to fish?

I promised I would.

You'll make his year, you know.

It's as if I don't want to fish. I miss it sometimes.

Do you?

I grew up on the water. Fishing is how my pa and I spent most of our Saturdays together. It brings back a lot of good memories, except instead of being the son, I get to be the pa this time.

He put an arm around Delia's waist and drew her closer so she was in his arms.

Does the ma want to kiss the pa?

Her heart raced with excitement. Well, that depends, she replied, deciding to be modest.

He raised an eyebrow. On what?

Is Pa going to bring home a fish for supper?

He can't guarantee it, but he'll do his best.

I suppose effort counts enough. Alright.

Ma will grant Pa a kiss.

He bowed his head to kiss her, and she held her breath in anticipation.

His lips brushed hers, sending a thrilling spark up and down her spine.

Besides the kiss he gave her at the courthouse, it'd been a long time since she kissed a man. She'd forgotten how wonderful it was. But it was better with Owen, for she knew he wasn't going to run off and leave her when things got tough.

For a moment, she thought he might end the kiss, but then he brought his lips back to hers and deepened it. In response, she wrapped her arms around his neck and pressed her body against his.

The thought did occur to her that perhaps she shouldn't be so eager. But then she remembered they were married, so it was perfectly fine for her to be enthusiastic with him.

He reached up to hold the side of her face with his hand.

Giving a light moan, she parted her lips for him and allowed him to pursue her more intimately.

He followed her silent lead and took his time in enjoying the moment. He was wonderfully solid against her.

His hands were gentle but firm. This was much better than kissing David had ever been. It was more than the fact that Owen wasn't rushing through the kiss to go further with her.

Owen was tender and patient. And best of all, he was her husband.

When he pulled back slightly, her heart was racing with the possibilities of what they might do.

Even if he couldn't consummates the marriage, there might be other things they could enjoy. But could a man really enjoy lovemaking without the ability to perform?

She thought to ask him about it when someone threw the front door open. She jerked, noting that Owen also gave a small jump, and breathed a sigh of relief when she saw Jeremy holding the stick in his hand.

There was that split second where she thought it might be David. She hadn't told Owen about David, but she knew she'd must...even if it would ruin the newfound joy, she'd found with her husband.

David had a way of causing problems.

I saw you come home, Pa!

Johnny exclaimed, as excited as a boy could be.

Yes, I did. Owen gave her waist a quick squeeze before he let her go.

I thought we might have our first fishing lesson.

His eyes grew wide. No kidding?

I didn't drag a boat all the way home to let it sit in the yard.

She gasped. You bought a boat?

Owen glanced at her and nodded. It's nothing fancy, but it'll do the job. That lake is deeper than it looks, and I think we might stand a better chance out there.

But that boat is a little heavy. I need someone strong to help me carry it. You have any ideas on who that someone might be?

Johnny puffed out his chest. I'm strong!

Well, you sure do look strong.

I am! I carried a box up the stairs all by myself when we moved in.

Chuckling, Owen winked at her. That's good enough proof for me. Let's go see if we can catch a fish for your ma to fry up.

Without a glance in her direction, Johnny bolted out the door and raced to the wagon which, did indeed, have a boat strapped to it.

He's a great kid. Owen gave her a quick kiss. Wish us luck!

As he headed toward the wagon, she called out, Good luck! and smiled as she watched them work together to get the boat onto the ground.

Reluctant, she closed the door so she could return to her sewing. Already, she missed being close to her husband.

That night, Owen was wide awake in bed, again aware of the fact that Delia was sleeping next to him.

It was a bittersweet experience to feel her soft body pressing up against him. She felt incredibly good, and the male part of him was insisting he nudge her and tell her that he could consummate this marriage.

But what if it was too soon? They'd only shared their first real kiss before he took Jeremy fishing.

Wasn't it jumping the gun to go from the kiss to ravishing her? He pushed the silly notion aside. He wouldn't ravishes her, no matter how eager his body was.

At least, he didn't think he would not when he was much too interested in checking out all of her.

Next time she dressed, he should barge into the room. It was natural that a wife dressed while in the presence of her husband.

In the past, he'd lost his nerve and didn't dare enter the room when she wasn't decent.

Well, he could thank his premarriage years of abstinence for that. Pre-marriage abstinence?

Being married hadn't changed his virginal status one single bit.

And this little fact was getting old fast.

There was no doubt about it. Irving Spencer had to overcome his problem. The kiss was a step in the right direction.

Next time they kissed, Owen would get a little further. He glanced at Delia in the moonlight.

Her eyes were shut, and her breathing was slow and even. Yep. She was asleep.

He wondered when they could do more than kiss.

Tomorrow? The next day? A week? He inwardly groaned. He really needed a plan.

If he established goals, then he might take note of his progress. Maybe that would help him be patient.

Letting out a low sigh, he debated getting up and doing something productive with his time. The leg of the chair in the kitchen needed to be sanded down so it wouldn't scratch the floor anymore.

He could work on that. But then he looked over at Delia who rolled onto her back. With the sheet at her waist, he had a pretty good view of her breasts because the nightgown she wore was a thin cotton material.

Fine. So, there was no way he was going to give up this to work on a chair leg, no matter how much his body was aching.

Instead, he rolled onto his side and stared at her. Whether he studied her angelic face or let his gaze drift lower, it didn't matter.

She was the most beautiful sight he'd ever beheld. Though, he had to admit, his focus seemed drawn more to her breasts than her face.

His fingers itched to touch her. Just what did breasts feel like anyway? Did he dare try to find out?

But that was wrong. He couldn't do that when she was asleep!

Even if they were married, he didn't feel right about taking that kind of liberty with her.

No. She'd have to be wide awake and aware of what was happening. However, watching her as she slept was fine. She chose to wear the nightgown to bed and lay down next to him.

Surely, she knew the chance she was taking in doing that. But would Irving Spencer even be interested in looking at her like this? Of course, he would. A man would have to be dead not to be interested.

He was very interested in her. She gave a soft sigh and opened her eyes.

Startled, he quickly directed his gaze from her breasts and up to her face.

To his surprise, she smiled and turned onto her side so she was facing him. Then she snuggled into his arms and rested her head against his chest.

His heart pounded with uncertainty. She hadn't done that before. At least, she hadn't wiggled up to him while she was awake.

What did it mean? What would Irving do? He'd want to caress her, wouldn't he?

A man in bed with a soft, warm body would want to hold her. Yes. That would be fine. He could hold her. He gingerly brought his arms around her.

She didn't protest. That was a good sign. Deciding to press his luck, he let his hand slide down her back. She wasn't angled in such a way where he could feel her breast, but he enjoyed tracing the curve of her hip.

She didn't protest that either. So that was something else he had permission to do. He didn't dare go further than that. Not tonight. This was enough.

Tomorrow, maybe he'd make a little more progress.

Patience, Owen. It'll come soon enough.

CHAPTER 10

At the Jailhouse

The next day at the jailhouse, Owen fell asleep while sorting through some paperwork.

Half aware he was dreaming; he gave himself permission to enjoy the world where anything could happen. He enjoys himself. He smiled at the images dancing before him.

Then, just when things got interesting between him and Delia, a loud bang jolted him from the world of sleep and back into the stark reality of unrelenting desire.

He blinked several times as he sat up in the chair and straightened his wrinkled vest. Then he adjusted his deputy badge and turned to the sheriff who gave him a knowing grin.

That little woman of yours keeping you up at night?

Well... Since the man had caught him sleeping on the job, Owen figured he might as well tell the truth, even if it was in a roundabout way. Yes.

Sheriff Meyer chuckled. There's nothing quite as wonderful as that first year of marriage. I'm glad things are working out between you two. She's a fine one. I knew you'd make her happy.

Uh...thanks. Owen wondered, once again, just how great this Irving Spencer really was. The man seemed to be idolized by everyone who heard his name.

In some ways, it was intimidating.

There was no way Owen could ever live up to that kind of legacy.

I got an assignment for you.

What is it?

I suspect that David is up to no good. He's supposed to be meeting up with some men in town.

Those men are shady characters. I haven't pinned anything on them yet, but my gut's telling me something is up with those three. I got word that they're meeting up at Guy Ike's house in an hour.

I'll give you directions and you can head on over to find out what they're talking about.

You mean, you want me to eavesdrop? Is that legal?

Don't eavesdrop. Just pass by a window and take a rock out of your boot.

Owen wondered if that was a good idea, but if there was something serious going on, then wouldn't it be better to find out exactly what that was?

Maybe he could prevent a bank robbery.

He nodded and stood up. Placing his hat on his head, he stretched.

David? Where have I heard that name before?

He's Johnny's father.

He stilled and stared at the sheriff. Johnny's father is in town?

I thought you knew. That's why you came to marry her.

I thought once you two exchanged vows, David would hightail it back to wherever he's been hiding for the past few years, but he won't leave.

That made Owen uncomfortable. Very uncomfortable.

He knew that Johnny had another father that another man had been with Delia, but it made him uneasy to know that this man was lingering around in town and that he'd have to deal with him.

If it was up to him, the man would stay out of sight forever.

The sheriff told him where to find Guy's house, patted him on the back and steered him to the front door.

Just stay there for a little while. There's no need to stay all afternoon.

Owen indicated his consent and left.

As he retrieved his horse from the post in front of the jailhouse, the boy he'd given the fishing rod to ran up to him.

Are you going to catch any outlaws today?

No. I'm afraid not today, Amos.

The boy looked disappointed.

Realizing the twelve-year-old was probably bored and needed an adventure, he said, but I do have an important task.

The boy's eyes lit up in interest. Oh?

Yes, but I can't tell anyone what it is.

Then he purposely paused to build the suspense. That is, of course, unless my partner promised to keep it a secret.

I can keep a secret!

Pretending to be alarmed, Owen glanced around and put his fingers to his lips.

Shhh... We need to be quiet. This is too important to mess up.

I'm sorry, he whispered, looking embarrassed. I won't be loud again.

Hiding his grin, Owen gave a slight nod. Good because this is a special mission. You see, there are some bad men who are planning something big.

How big?

I don't know. That's what I must find out. He tipped his hat back and gave the boy a good look, as if trying to make a difficult decision.

Are you any good at listening?

I sure am.

And can you be quiet?

Uh huh.

As quiet as a mouse?

Yes.

Great. Then you can be my partner. He held his hand out. This makes it official.

Excited, Amos shook his hand. Should I bring the fishing rod?

Though Owen didn't think they'd need one, he decided it might be fun if the boy had a weapon with him.

That's a great idea. You never know when you'll need something like that.

I'll be back. The boy began to run off but then turned to ask, you won't leave without me, will you?

No. I'll wait.

While the boy went to retrieve the rod, Owen saddled up his horse. As soon as he finished, the boy returned and, sure enough, he had the fishing rod with him.

I don't have a horse, he said.

Owen shrugged. I got one and this saddle will fit the two of us. Hop on.

He obeyed and they headed off for Guy's house. Once he had the horse tied to a tree where no one would easily spot it, the two made their way to the rundown barn.

Does Guy live here? Owen whispered.

Sometimes. Usually, he runs off with his brother Jimmy.

To do what?

A little bit of gambling and running odd jobs.

Owen stopped to take a good look at the twelve-year-old.

Just how much did this kid know? You have any idea what they'd want with David?

Well, my ma said that David wanted his son back, but you came in the nick of time and stopped that.

That much Owen already knew. Still... How does your ma know that?

She cuts hair and takes in laundry. People talk to her.

Apparently. You got anything else on David?

He shrugged. Not really. He ran off a good few year ago and now he's back.

Owen nodded. At least that was something to go on.

They reached the two-story house before the four men arrived on the land.

When they saw the men, they scooted around to the side of the house so they wouldn't be spotted.

Once the men got into the house and slammed the door, one of them opened a window. Seeing this as a good opportunity to better hear them, Owen motioned for the boy to join him and crawled to the other end of the house.

It's hotter than the pit of hell in here, one of them gruffly said.

Hasn't been living in since June. What'd you expect? another replied.

Who cares? Let's get down to business. We're stuck in a rock and a hard place. How're we going to get out?

One grunted. If David would have followed through, we'd be fine.

It's not my fault. Obviously, that was David, and the voice sounded familiar.

Owen had to know where he'd seen David before. He eased up from the ground and peeked through the open window.

It is your fault! a scruffy man barked. If that damn deputy stayed away, we'd be sitting' pretty on our way west.

Stan didn't come through, David said.

Alright. Now Owen knew what David looked like, and he remembered seeing him before. But where? One of the men turned in his direction, so Owen quickly sat back down.

His heart pounded anxiously. Did the man see him?

Stan did come through alright. What'd you are going to do about it?

What can I do? David asked. We had a deal, and he blew it. It's not my problem anymore.

Another man butted in. We got news for you, Jenkins.

It's still your problem. No money? You got problems.

There was a slight ruckus before someone ran up the steps.

After him!

There was a rush to obey him, and Owen wondered if everyone was upstairs. He got up and peeked into the window.

The room was empty, but he heard shouts and gunshots from upstairs. Turning to the boy, Owen nodded to the fishing rod.

How good are you with that?

Real good. I've been practicing.

Think you can get that wallet over there in the middle of the room?

There was no way he was going to risk the boy going in there, and he wasn't small enough to fit through the window.

The boy stood up and looked through the open window.

Oh sure. That's nothing.

Those men might be upstairs now, but at any moment, they were bound to return. They'd have to act fast, and he knew this would be the highlight of the boy's day if he was the one to get the wallet. He patted the boy on the back.

Go ahead and fish it out of there but be quick. Those men won't stay up there forever.

You think it has something important in it?

He shrugged. There's only one way to find out.

The boy nodded.

Owen lifted the boy so half of his body fit into the window. The boy surprised Owen because he did, indeed, catch the wallet on the first try. Great job, he cheered as loud as he dared.

Fortunately, the gunshots and commotion made it easy to mask any other sounds. Now, reel it in.

The boy obeyed, and Owen set him back down. That was fun!

Shhhh....

Sorry.

Owen saw some debt notes and a piece of paper. He lifted the paper out and saw, Robert Scott and Farewell Bank.

October 23rd. 12:30. He read the items several times before he placed the paper back into the wallet and handed it to the boy.

Throw it back in.

Don't you want to keep it? the boy asked.

No. They'll suspect something if it's missing. He lifted the boy and let him throw it back into the room.

Good. Let's get out of here.

They made it to Owen's horse right before two men ran out of the house. Owen hid the boy behind a tree and grabbed his gun.

True, he didn't know how to use it at least not well enough to hit his mark but if anyone found them, he'd give it his best shot.

Fortunately, the two men didn't go in their direction.

They hopped on their horses and rode off. Owen breathed a sigh of relief. Good. They were safe.

The boy peered around the tree. Did you see the other Two?

No. And that gave Owen a bad feeling. He saw David leave since he was one of the men who ran out of there. He didn't recognize the other one.

He glanced at the boy. Do you hear anything?

The boy shook his head.

It shouldn't be that quiet in there. Something was wrong.

He had to investigate. Stay here. I'll be back.

Those are dangerous men in there!

The kid had a point a good one but, I'm the deputy.

It's my job to face danger. Even if he was scared. Irving wouldn't be scared.

He was, after all, the picture of courage, but Irving wasn't here. Owen was. And that meant Owen had to take charge.

Forcing aside his unease, he cleared his throat. You promise me you'll stay here and be good.

The boy nodded.

Owen made his way to the house, careful to be quiet so he could hear any noise in case he needed to hide. But no noise came.

It was quiet. Very quiet. His hands trembled. Oh boy.

This was a far cry from fishing!

Wiping his sweaty hands on his pants, he renewed a firm grasp on the gun and held it out.

As long as he directed it where a threat came up at him, he might hit his target...or at least scare the other man enough so he could get away.

One glance in the boy's direction assured him that the boy was still safe and out of the way.

Owen rounded the corner of the house and cautiously stepped onto the porch. Still quiet.

There were only two options as to why it'd be this silent. One, the men knew he was there and were waiting for him.

That thought made him tighten his grip on the Colt .45. The men could be injured or dead. There had been an awful lot of gunshots while he and the boy were getting that wallet.

Someone could easily have gotten hurt. He cringed.

He didn't want to see a dead body.

Well, either way, he was about to find out. He could do this. He was pretending to be Irving Spencer.

All he had to do was imitate the man. Straightening his shoulders and scowling in his best. I'm a tough man imitation, he entered the house through the open door.

No one was in the room. There was a battered old couch and a wooden table with two chairs.

That was it for furniture, and there were no long curtains to hide behind. It was a small house.

Smaller than the one he and Delia had. Delia Just the thought of her beautiful smile made him second guess whether he wanted to risk his life like this. But he had to.

He was the deputy. Just pretend you're Irving and everything will be fine.

Strengthened, he pressed forward.

As he reached the bottom step of the narrow staircase, he remembered the wallet. Glancing over his shoulder, he realized that the wallet was gone. So, one of those two men took it on their way out the door.

Well, it was a good thing he thought to return it.

He directed his gaze to the top of the stairs. Still no sound. He took his first step and ducked when he heard a noise.

He waited but nothing happened. As soon as he realized that he caused the creak when he pressed his foot onto the step, he sighed with relief. Thank goodness. No one was shooting at him.

He really needed to get a grip on being the deputy. No deputy could afford to be a chicken cowering at the slightest noise.

He looked behind him. Good. The room was still empty, and from what he could tell from looking out the two windows and door, no one had returned.

He resumed his walk up the steps, careful to be as quiet as the old steps allowed, and paused when he reached the top.

There was a narrow hallway with two rooms. There was also a broken kerosene lamp and table between the two rooms.

Bullet holes marked the walls too. Yep. There had been a shoot-out up here.

He held his breath and waited. Still, no noise. They could be waiting for him in one of those bedrooms. He thought of the best way to proceed.

Catching sight of a shard of glass from the lamp, he picked it up and flung it into one of the bedrooms.

Nothing.

So that meant the men had to be dead, right? After all, one would have shot if he was startled.

At least, Owen hoped so. He moved forward and stopped when he reached the bedrooms, which were directly opposite one another. He noticed the blood on the floor before he saw the two men, lying face down.

They didn't move. They didn't even blink. But their eyes were open and it spooked him.

Though they were most likely dead, he had the creepy I'm being watched feeling.

Giving a slight shiver, he entered the room they were in.

He knew they were dead. Well, he was 99% sure. But he knew he had to check. Blood seeped out of their sides and chest.

One was even shot in the neck. He fought the urge to vomit. He'd never seen so much blood in his entire life, except for when he gutted fish...and that was a completely different scenario than the one confronting him now.

He closed his eyes and took a deep breath. Big mistake.

Now he was aware of the foul smell soaking from the bodies.

He quickly ran over to the window and opened it. He leaned out and inhaled the fresh air. There was nothing like the cool autumn breeze to calm a man's stomach.

He caught sight of the boy and waved to him. Then, in case the other two decided to return, he indicated that he was alright.

The boy nodded and, thankfully, stayed put.

Owen braced himself for the images of the men and turned to face them. The second time looking at them wasn't much easier than the first.

Swallowing the bitterness that rose in his throat, he quickly made his way over to them and tapped them with his foot. Neither one budged.

That was enough proof for him. He wasn't about to feel for a pulse. He couldn't imitate Irving that well yet!

Relieved, he raced out of the house to notify the sheriff about this turn of events.

CHAPTER 11

David's Mom

Two hours later, Delia was working on a baby gown for one of the better well-to-do new mothers in town when a loud rapping at the door made her bolt in surprise. She accidently pricked her finger with the needle.

Ouch. She sucked on her finger and set aside the thimble and clothing so she could answer the door.

Johnny got up from where he was playing with his toys and followed her.

Delia's heart raced at the rapid pounding at the door. Did something happen to Owen or one of her siblings? There was no denying that whoever was on the other end considered their visit to be an emergency.

Who is it, Ma?

I don't know, honey. She could have checked through the window, but she didn't want to waste the extra couple of seconds that it would require.

She opened the door and gasped when she saw David's mother standing in front of her with a glare on her face.

My son is not a killer! the woman yelled before could speak.

I wasn't sure she heard right. What?

The woman barged into the house, pushing past both Delia and Johnny.

Where's that no good husband of yours?

Johnny put her hands over Jeremy's ears. I will not have you are talking about Irving that way, especially not in front of his son.

Irving Spencer is not she motioned to Jeremy that child's father.

Her face grew hot with anger. His name is Johnny.

I didn't come here to talk about him.

Of course not! The woman didn't care one single bit about her own grandchild. Delia turned to her son and said, go upstairs and play with your toys. And close the door.

He didn't need to hear anything else that viper of a woman had to say. Ma must take care of some things, alright?

He nodded and obediently went up the stairs.

Delia waited until he closed the door before she glared at David's mother. You have no right to barge into my home.

The woman crossed her arms. Well, that fool husband of yours has no right to accuse David of murder.

Murder?

And don't think for a minute that I can't connect the dots, missy. She pointed her finger in Delia's face. You managed to weasel your way out of letting David be with his son, and now you're using your husband who just happens to be the Deputy to put Clyde away for good.

I have no idea what you're talking about.

Oh really? You mean to tell me you don't know that Sheriff Meyer arrested David?

No. But if he did, then David deserved it. The woman huffed. I shouldn't be surprised that you'd say that. You've had it in for David ever since you first laid eyes on him.

I'm not having this conversation with you again. Delia stormed over to the door and pointed outside. Get out of here!

Not until you release David.

That's not my decision! Glaring at the woman, she flung her hand toward the doorway and hit something solid. She quickly looked at what she smacked and saw Owen. Oh! I'm sorry. I didn't know you were there.

Humph! David's mother grumbled. I don't care if you are the deputy, Irving Spencer. You have no right to go around arresting anyone just because this hussy exchanges sexual favors for you to do her dirty work.

Now, that's out of line, Owen snapped. Delia's my wife and I won't have you talking about her that way. Just what has you fit to be tied anyway?

You know, she replied. You got my boy arrested.

I've gotten three men arrested since I got here. Which boy' are you referring to Delia?

The one you just tossed into jail!

Well, someone killed Guy and Jimmy, and David and Joshua were the only ones there at the house. I saw all of them with my own eyes, and I heard the gunshots.

The sheriff wants to hold him long enough to find out if he killed Guy or Jimmy.

They're still looking for Joshua. If David's innocent, he'll go free.

No! the woman protested, frantically shaking her head.

I order you to release him at once. He's innocent!

The law doesn't work that way. I saw David in that house. I know he was there.

This is personal, she insisted. It has nothing to do with the law. She glared at Jenny. Isn't it enough that you won't let me or my son near his own child? Must you frame him for murder too?

Keep Jenny out of this, Owen said, standing in front of Jenny as if to protect her. It has nothing to do with her.

You don't want to see Johnny any more than David does, Delia hissed, edging around Owen so she could approach the old coot.

Just why is David so interested in Johnny all the sudden anyway?

She lifted her chin and crossed her arms. He's always been interested. It's just that you refused to have anything to do with him.

You seduced him until you got with child, and then your brothers chased him out of town. He wanted to do right by you and marry you, but you wouldn't let him. None of you would. And now you're determined to put him away for good, if he doesn't get hanged first.

David shouldn't have been hanging around where he didn't belong. Delia glanced at Owen. What happened?

A shoot-out, most likely.

She turned back to Clyde's irate mother. There you go.

What was he doing in a shoot-out anyway? Something was wrong with the whole picture, and Jenny wished she could figure it out.

There was no way would take a sudden interest in Delia.

And now he was having a shoot-out with... Who did you say got killed? she asked Owen.

Guy and Johnny.

Her eyes grew wide. Guy and Ike?

He nodded.

She rolled her eyes. No wonder got put into prison if he was hanging around those shady characters. She turned to the woman.

Aren't you aware that Guy and Jimmy are...I mean, were...dangerous? If was with them, then he was up to no good.

And just what did that have to do with Johnny? Was there a connection or was it a coincidence?

Owen took off his hat and hung it up by the door. Mrs. Diaz, this is my house.

Delia didn't welcome you here and neither do I. Leave before I get you for trespassing.

Delia couldn't help but give a slight grin of satisfaction as David's mother grudgingly made her way out the front door. It was nice to have a man and a deputy, no less to put the old bat in her place.

The woman didn't care about Johnny any more than David did.

Not once in all the time she'd had him did either David or his mother came to see him.

Relieved when Owen finally shut the door, she thanked him and turned to the staircase.

Why don't you let me talk to him, Owen suggested.

She glanced over her shoulder. I try to keep him away from all of this.

She motioned to the closed door. It can't be easy on him to know that there are people who should care about him but don't.

He walked over to her and took her hand in his. You're right. It can't. And children pick up more than adults realize.

Sometimes a boy needs a man he can talk to.

Sighing, she realized he was right. All these years Johnny had needed a father in his life, and now that he had one, she needed to let the father do his job.

Alright. He gave her hand a gentle squeeze and kissed her. He's a good kid. You've done a great job with him. But you have help now.

She smiled. And good help it is.

He let go of her hand and turned to the staircase. Maybe I'll take him out to the lake. It's not that cold out today.

If you catch anything, I'll fry it up.

Sounds like a deal.

Owen? she called as he climbed the steps.

He glanced back at her.

Will you tell me what happened today when everything settles down?

Yep.

Nodding her thanks, she returned to her sewing.

The next day, Delia took Johnny to the jailhouse so her son could see Owen at work.

As soon as she opened the door, she caught him sorting through some Wanted posters. He stiffened and quickly turned to them. His eyes were wide.

She laughed. Relax. It's just us.

He gave a half-hearted chuckle before he straightened the stack.

Uh...just checking on the outlaws.

I hope you get them all, she replied, admiring the way he looked in his denims and vest with the shiny deputy badge on it.

She smiled when she saw the fishing rod leaning against the wall.

Sure, his methods were unorthodox, but from what she heard, he managed.

Maybe that was why he earned himself an all-star reputation back in South Carolina. She scanned the length of the building and frowned. I thought David was here.

He sighed. He was. The sheriff caught Joshua this morning, and it turns out Joshua did the actual shooting. So David was released. Joshua was sent to his hometown where he's wanted.

She nodded. She shouldn't be surprised. David didn't strike her as someone brave enough to handle a weapon, but it had made her feel a little better knowing he wasn't running free through town.

She glanced at Johnny and squeezed his hand.

Children had no control over their circumstances, and they seemed to handle things well enough.

She just hoped that with Owen to take David's place, Johnny would have an easier time of it.

Did you come for a tour? Owen asked, walking over to them.

We were in town and thought we'd say hello, she replied. What do you think, Johnny? Do you want to see where Pa works?

The boy eagerly nodded, so Owen put him up on his shoulders.

Here is Sheriff Meyer's desk. I share it with him.

She motioned to the stack of paperwork. It looks like you do a lot more than catch dangerous men.

Yep. Judges and lawyers like reports.

That made sense.

Over here, he began as he directed them to the three cells, is where we keep the prisoners.

Whoa! Johnny said when they stopped in front of an empty cell. Do bad men go in there?

worse than others. We get the occasional drunk or bar brawler.

Do you get bank robbers?

Sometimes.

I want to see a bank robber!

Well, you would have if we didn't stop the robbery.

Johnny's eyes grew wide. You did?

Just the other day. Someone was going to rob Farewell Bank. The sheriff and I got there before the robbers did.

Did you see the robbers?

Owen shrugged. I'm sure we did, but we aren't sure which of the men who entered were supposed to do it. They probably saw us and left.

And there's been no attempts on the bank since then?

Delia asked.

Nope. We're keeping a lookout. Right now, all I have is a name, Owen replied. Does the name Robert Scott ring a bell?

She shook her head. I've never heard that one before.

Probably an out-of-towner then. I'm guessing he has connections with someone in town though.

I want to be a deputy when I grow up! Johnny said, obviously impressed.

He chuckled as he turned from the bars. Over here is where we make coffee and heat up the place.

He patted the potbelly stove in the corner with his free hand. Over there is where we hang our coats and hats. And over here is where we play checkers when we get bored.

The sheriff and deputy get bored when there's that stack of papers on the desk? Delia asked, amused by the quaint spot for games.

He shrugged and grinned. Everyone needs a break.

Do you and the sheriff get along?

Well, enough. I have no complaints about working with him.

He obviously adores you, she said. I remember before you got here, and he couldn't stop bragging on you. He kept saying you were the best deputy in South Carolina and that you'd be good to me and Johnny.

She reached out and touched his arm.

He was right. I'm glad you came.

His easy smile faltered. Right.

She wondered at the change in his mood.

He lifted the boy off his shoulders and placed him down.

Why don't you go check out the checkerboard. You can stack the pieces.

Johnny ran to the board and started collecting the black pieces.

And don't put any of them in your mouth, Delia added before she went to Owen.

Leaning close to him, she whispered, Is something wrong?

He let out a slow breath and directed his gaze to her.

Well... You and Johnny mean everything to me. You know that, don't you?

Now she was worried. What is it? Did something bad happen? Not that she could imagine what that something could possibly be, but still... He was a deputy. Maybe someone wanted to come after him.

She clenched her hands together at the thought of some angry thief coming after Owen with a loaded gun. Why hadn't she considered that aspect of his job before?

I should tell you something.

She closed her eyes and braced herself. Is someone out to kill you? What?

She opened her eyes and looked at him. Did one of those terrible bank robbers get loose and decide to track you down?

A bank robber? The confusion left his face as her meaning dawned on him. Oh. No. It has nothing to do with that.

She relaxed. What a relief. For a minute there, I thought your life was in danger.

He squinted and glanced at the ceiling. Well, I guess you could say...

The door opened and the sheriff walked in. Howdy, he greeted, tipping his hat in her direction. It's nice to see everyone together.

We just stopped by to say hi, Delia assured him. We don't intend to take up any more of your deputy's time.

She gave Owen a quick kiss. I'm glad you're safe. I'll see you at home.

She motioned to Johnny.

Come on, honey. We need to go see your Aunt Sandy about Saturday.

Owen nodded, looking both relieved and disappointed.

Sure. I'll even dress up in those fancy clothes the sheriff bought me for our wedding day.

Thank you, Owen. She took Johnny's hand, and on her way out of the jailhouse, she said good-bye to the sheriff.

CHAPTER 12

The Romantic Dinner

Delia bit her lower lip as she studied at the parlor. If this didn't peak Rick's romantic interest, then he was a lost cause.

She spent that entire Saturday getting everything ready for the special supper.

The lacy white curtains were drawn to give the room a private feel to it, and she had set out the matching tablecloth. She made both years ago when she thought she'd marry David.

Was she ever glad she ended up with Owen instead!

She hummed as she lit the two candles. She dimmed the kerosene lamp and smiled.

Though she had no flowers, she arranges some colorful leaves in the center of the table and placed a pinecone on top of it. Closing her eyes, she inhaled the sweet scent, which was almost masked by the pot roast that was cooling in the oven.

She opened her eyes and set the cushions on the chairs so they'd be comfortable.

Then she stepped back and examined the effect of the candlelight. It seemed magical to be in here. She clapped her hands and nearly skipped out of the room. Owen and Johnny waited in the kitchen.

As she requested, they dressed up for the occasion. Even she wore her best shirt and skirt.

I feel fancy, Johnny said, beaming.

Yep, Owen agreed. This is just like those restaurants where rich people eat.

Let's hope it does the trick! She was too excited to sit down, so she checked the dinner rolls. Fresh and soft. Perfect.

She glanced at the two men who sat on the remaining chairs she had left in the kitchen when she moved the table and other chairs to the parlor.

She smiled at them. Thank you for doing this.

Owen grinned and patted his stomach. It's the least we can do since you're letting us feast on this meal too.

You even made cake! Johnny cheered, bouncing in his seat.

She chuckled at her son's enthusiasm. That I did.

We can't wait to dig in, Owen replied.

There was a knock at the door.

She gave a brief shout of glee before she ran to the door and opened it.

Come on in! She told Sandy, Rick, and Greg.

You weren't kidding, Sandy, Rick said as he helped her take off her coat.

This place really is nice. He turned to the hook by the door and hung it up. You did good, Delia.

Delia laughed.

I can't take all the credit. Owen had something to do with it. She glanced at Owen who stood up.

Well, it was the sheriff, Owen said. He had this house in tip top shape when we moved in.

How is he doing? Rick asked as he shrugged off his own coat.

He's fine. I notice he works all the time, Owen replied.

Rick hung the coat up and took Greg's coat to put on another hook. I heard he's all business. Yes, he is.

Delia cleared her throat to get their attention. It worked.

She motioned to the parlor.

Rick and Sally, will you follow me?

Rick peered into the other room. Wow. You didn't have to go through all this trouble for us.

Sandy ran on ahead and looked over at Delia with unconcealed enthusiasm in her eyes.

It's lovely, Delia. You must have spent hours on this.

Not really, Dela said.

The supper took longer, but I want you two to have a wonderful and relaxing evening. So tonight, let Owen, the kids, and I handle everything.

She went over to one of the chairs and pulled it out.

Sandy?

Her sister readily obeyed.

Rick shook his head and grinned. It is a nice thing to do for us, Delia. Thank you.

You're welcome. Satisfied, she added, we'll be serving you shortly. Then she left and went to the kitchen. Are we ready?

Greg and Johnny stood at attention and nodded.

She laughed. You don't have to be so formal, but I do appreciate the enthusiasm.

He grabbed the utensils and plates and held them out to the boys.

Be careful with these. We know, Greg said. He loosened his tie a bit before he took the plates.

She gave the utensils to Johnny and watched as they went to the parlor.

Owen picked up the bottle of wine and champagne glasses.

You really thought of everything.

I had days to plan for it. She lifted the salad bowl and joined him on his way to the parlor.

After the boys set out their items, she served the salad while Owen poured the wine in their glasses.

Potato soup is next, she said.

My favorite, Rick replied.

And you make it better than I do, Sandy told her.

I like your soup too, Rick said.

I know, but Jenny knows exactly how much cheese to add. She has a gift for making potato soup.

Delia finished dishing out their portions of salad. I thank both of you.

Once she returned to the kitchen with Owen, she realized Greg and Johnny were staring at the ceiling and talking about a strange noise.

What is it? she asked, setting the bowl down.

Greg pointed up. We heard something scurrying around up there.

She frowned. But the dog's outside. She inwardly shivered. What if it was a mouse? She hated those things!

I'll check it out, Owen said as he turned to the staircase.

No, Greg said. It's sounds like it's coming from the roof.

Oh. Owen stopped to listen.

They stood in silence for a moment before another series of pitter patters drifted down to them. It wasn't on the roof, but it was somewhere up there. She glanced uneasily at Owen. The attic?

I think so.

Oh gross! A rodent was running around in their home!

When she saw him begin to walk up the stairs, she yelled out, Wait!

He turned to her.

She went to a shelf and retrieved an empty flour sack. If you catch it, you might as well put it in here. How she hoped he'd be quick about getting it and throwing it out of the house!

She ran over to him and handed it to him before she gave him a quick kiss. For luck.

There's nothing to it. I used to drive out snakes at my aunt's house.

She nodded. I hope it's as easy to get as a snake.

I'm sure it'll be. He ran up the stairs.

Turning to the boys, she said, this is one time when I'm really glad to have a man in the house.

Sandy directed her attention to Rick as she finished her salad. I had no idea she'd do all of this. She was deeply touched that her sister went out of her way to make this a memorable evening.

I feel underdressed. He glanced down at his suit. And this is what I wear to church.

You look as good in it as you did two years ago when you bought it.

He looked at her with a twinkle in his eye. Well, you are absolutely beautiful.

She blushed. It'd been a long time since he told her that.

Delia, it seemed, had a wonderful idea.

The atmosphere was not only romantic, but it was enchanting as well. It was as if the hands of time were rewound, and she was the same youth who let Rick court her.

She sipped her wine and furrowed her eyebrows. She glanced at Rick and then looked up. Is there something going on up there?

It certainly sounds like it.

Delia entered with two bowls of soup and placed them on the table.

Are the boys playing? Sandy asked.

No, Delia answered. There's something in the attic so Irving went to investigate.

Sandy blushed. I hope he gets it.

You and me both.

Does he need help? Rick asked, ready to stand up.

Delia motioned for him to sit back down. He said he's handled critters before, so he'll be fine. You two need to enjoy the meal...and try to ignore the activity up there.

If you're sure... Rick sounded uncertain.

Of course, I'm sure. He's very capable. Now I'm going to bring the roast and gravy out.

Alright.

Delia picked up the plates and left the room.

Sandy had to admit her sister was going above and beyond the call of duty to give her and Rick a romantic meal, and she couldn't think of a time when she loved her sister more.

She could only hope that she might return the favor sometime.

The loud thump above their heads made her jump. She laughed.

That must be some rodent up there.

He set the spoon down and sighed. I don't feel right sitting here while he's up there fighting that thing.

Delia said he can handle it. We should enjoy the meal she made for us. She picked up the spoon and dipped it into the soup. She took a bite and smiled. This is the best potato soup anyone's ever made.

Rick sighed as something small ran on the ceiling above them. He doesn't sound like he's having much success.

She groaned and set the spoon down. Will you please let him take care of it? The man's caught snakes before.

I can help him and then come back down here.

Why is it that every time we get a moment to ourselves, you run off to do something else? Am I that burdensome to you?

He rolled his eyes. Not this again. Come on, Sandy. This isn't work related, alright?

Delia said Irving can do this by himself. Let him take care of it.

Another rumble of noise echoed from the attic. He's not taking care of it!

Yes, he is!

You hear that up there? How can you call that he is taking care of it?

Tonight, is supposed to be about you and me. You promised, Rick.

Do you really want him to suffer through all that?

Delia quickly grabbed the platter full of neatly cut pot roast and hurried into the parlor, hoping to stop her sister and her husband from fighting.

Is something wrong? she anxiously called out as she entered the room.

Yes, Delia, there is. Tears filled Sandy's eyes as she stood up. Rick doesn't love me anymore. He'd rather be up there chasing a stupid rodent than be down here with me.

That's not true, he said, his face red with anger. He threw his cloth napkin down and stood up.

Oh really? Then why do you avoid me all the time? She demanded, hands on her hips.

I must work. If I don't, I can't put food on the table.

You do more than your share of work. You're doing others' work too.

Townsend's been sick!

He's not the only one you fill in for. You also do some of the clerk's duties.

Because he was fired.

Then hire someone!

I can't, Rick argued. It's not my position.

Then talk to your boss or have someone else help you.

In a desperate attempt to break up their argument, Delia motioned to the roast.

This is getting cold. Now, Irving can do this. He's got everything under control!

In that instant, a crack came from the ceiling before it caved in, and Owen fell onto the table. Sandy screamed as a bowl of soup landed on her dress. One of the candles landed on Owen, and he caught on fire. Delia dropped the roast.

I'll go to the well! Greg yelled as he ran to the door and flung it open.

Delia and Sandy grabbed the candles and blew them out.

Rick took the tablecloth and beat it on the place where Owen's shirt was in small flames. The dog bolted into the house, barking, and running on top of Owen.

Delia reached for the dog and pulled him off Owen.

Stop it! she scolded the animal. As soon as the fire was out, she pulled off Owen's shirt. I think the wounds are minor.

She glanced at Sandy and Rick who looked bewildered. Do you think we should take him to the doctor?

I'm fine, Delia, Owen assured her. It shocked me more than it hurt.

Are you sure? She inspected his red skin.

Yes, I'm sure.

Greg came in with a pail of water. He looked disappointed. Oh, the fire's out already?

Through the hole in the ceiling, a squirrel leapt in front of Delia. She jumped onto Owen's lap and shrieked.

The dog, who'd been eating portions of the roast, stopped, and barked at the critter.

The squirrel ran under the chair. The dog ran after it and knocked the chair over. The two animals went in circles around the room twice before the squirrel found the exit and bolted out the front door.

The dog followed it right on outside, leaving everyone in shock.

This is all your fault! Rick told Sandy.

Sandy's jaw dropped. My fault?

Yes. If you'd let me, go up there and help him, none of this would have happened.

You don't know that!

It wouldn't have hurt to try.

Oh please. The only thing that would have been different is that both of you would have fallen through the ceiling instead of just one.

Rick looked as if he couldn't believe his ears. Are you saying that I'm incompetent?

Sandy raised an eyebrow and crossed her arms. Are you saying he's incompetent? She nodded in Owen's direction.

Of course not. There's your answer.

Delia sighed. Apparently, the romantic mood she'd carefully set up had been destroyed. She helped Owen to his feet and said, I'm sorry, Sandy and Rick. I never meant it to be this way.

Owen coughed before adding. I would have fallen through whether you were there or not, Rick. The floor up there was thin.

It doesn't matter, Sandy said, obviously irritated. The point is he'd rather be up there chasing a stupid animal than spending time with me. Just like he'd rather be doing anything if it doesn't involve me!

That's not true! Rick argued.

Sandy rushed to the door, and the others followed. She snatched her coat off the hook and hurriedly put it on.

Greg ran over to her. Does this mean I can't stay here tonight?

I don't think so, sweetheart, she told her son.

Why not? Rick asked. We already promised him he could.

She glared at him. And you promised to love and cherish me above all others but look at how well that turned out!

He groaned and threw his hands up in the air. What does that have to do with Greg staying here?

There's no need for him to stay because nothing interesting will happen at home. She grabbed Greg's coat and put it on him. Let's go, honey.

Glancing at Delia and Owen, she gave an apologetic smile. Thank you both for a wonderful meal. Then she headed out with Greg.

Rolling his eyes, Rick snatched his coat and said, we'll see you at church.

The door shut and Delia sighed. That didn't go at all like she hoped.

Owen put his arm around her shoulders and gave her a slight squeeze. It's alright.

Johnny, who had stayed out of the way during the ordeal, stepped from the corner of the parlor. Don't cry, Ma. I can clean.

That's a good idea, Owen quickly said. We'll clean up this mess. I'm sure Rick and Sandy will work things out.

She supposed he was right. But she really wished things could have ended better.

CHAPTER 13

Owen's Burn

Delia wiped ointment on Owen's arms to soothe his burns. As she did, he watched her, enjoying the way she fussed over him.

His Aunt Rachel had fussed over him too, but it was different with Delia. It was much nicer. He was lying on the bed and she sat next to him, gentle and caring.

Yes. It was much nicer.

She closed the lid on the jar and placed it on the nightstand.

Then she wiped her hand on a clean cloth. It was funny...in a way.

What? Seeing me on fire?

No, silly. She nudged him playfully in the side. That a squirrel could cause so much damage.

He chuckled. That was a smart squirrel. She got up.

He tried to reach for her hand to stop her, but she was too quick for him. Quick just like the squirrel. Where are you going? To check on Johnny.

He watched as she left the room. It was unfortunate that things happened as they did. Delia had been so excited about making the perfect supper, and all it took was a loose squirrel in the attic to spoil everything. She had a good heart. He lucked out when he married her.

Well, maybe Owen Russell didn't luck out. It was Irving Spencer who did. He sighed and pushed the stab of guilt aside.

So, he took on another name. Did that make him horrible person? He winced and rubbed his forehead. But what else was he supposed to do?

Turn himself in? Who would believe he had killed to protect himself when Big Roy and his men claimed otherwise?

Big Roy was an imposing force. He even got the law involved. And now Owen was part of that law. Though he couldn't denies the irony of the situation, he wished it hadn't happened like this.

He wished he hadn't married Jenny under these conditions. When he kept busy, it was easy to forget his deception.

But when he fell through the attic floor, his life passed before his eyes. He used to think people saying that happened were exaggerating... except they weren't.

It really was that profound and quick. Delia hadn't married a brave deputy ready to take on all the outlaws in the world. Nope. She married a fisherman who had lived a relatively quiet and peaceful life in the Louisiana swamp until he decided to get Aunt Rachel's money back. That decision led him into a whole lot of trouble.

Would Delia blame him if she knew? He could imagine her disappointment when she discovered he wasn't the strong, invincible Irving Spencer. He could see the sheriff's angry allow when he realized he'd been had by a simple fisherman.

Then, there was Johnny. That was probably the hardest one to deal with. In some ways, the boy looked up to him as if he were a hero. Owen had never been a hero before. The last thing he wanted to do was disappoint that little boy. Just how could he tell Jeremy he was a fraud?

Delia returned to their bedroom and shut the door. He's asleep. Owen nodded and swallowed the lump in his throat. He loved that boy with the same love his pa probably loved him with.

He always wanted Johnny to be proud of him.

What a day, huh? she asked, breaking him out of his thoughts.

He turned his head, and his eyes grew wide.

Was she going to undress in front of him?

She removed her shirt. I hope they'll be in a better mood when we see them at church tomorrow.

He blinked. Who? Oh right. Sandy and Rick. She was still talking about them. You can't change anything by worrying about it.

She glanced at him and sighed. You're right. I'm sure they'll get through it.

He was ready to voice his agreement when she slipped out of her skirt. Now, his interest was peaked. Was she going to keep taking her clothes off? He'd always gone to bed after she got ready for the night.

Apparently, he should have made it a point to come into the bedroom earlier in the evenings.

She went over to the kerosene lamp, and he feared that she'd turn down the flame, but she didn't. She simply took her necklace off and laid it on the dresser.

He breathed a sigh of relief. That was close. He didn't want to miss this for a moment. She took off another layer of clothing, and he couldn't believe she had more underneath.

Did women have to wear all those undergarments every day? The whole process of watching her, and her not seeming to even notice he was in the same room or simply forward about being in his viewing range, was as frustrating as it was arousing.

He wanted to see if she'd bare everything, but the suspense was thrilling, to say the least. He couldn't remember a time when he'd been more entertained in his entire life.

By the time he finally got to see her breasts, he had to physically close his mouth. Thankfully, she didn't notice. It would be embarrassing if he showed just how eager he was to see her naked. Sure, this was the greatest thing that ever happened to him, but he didn't have to let her know that.

She removed the last of her clothing, and he was as excited as a little kid who just caught his first big fish. He had to stop himself from jumping up and down on the bed. He knew that women looked good without clothes on, but he had no idea just how good they looked.

They were beautiful. He wished he could take this moment and gaze at her forever. But in the split second he got to see her completely nude, she then turned to the dresser drawer to select a clean undergarment to put on.

No! In his panic, he grabbed his arms and said, Ouch!...

She gasped and turned to him, dropping the piece of clothing that would block his view of her, and ran over to him a process that he most enjoyed since her perky breasts bounced.

This was a lot more fun than sitting in a boat and waiting for a fish to reel in. Remembering his arms, he gave a slight wince, trying to look brave through the pain, and said, maybe I need more ointment.

She nodded and grabbed the jar. He struggled not to stare at her breasts, but every time he forced his gaze to her face, it ended up falling back down.

She took his arm and placed it on her lap as she dug into the jar.

His fingertips brushed her thigh. Her skin was so incredibly soft. He sighed. Yes. He could get used to this.

Delia, he whispered.

What? she asked, gently rubbing ointment on his arm.

I'm glad I'm your husband. A man couldn't ask for a better wife.

She looked at him then and smiled. I'm glad you came to marry me.

Supported by her confession, he scooted closer to her and wrapped his arm around her waist, pulling her against him. I love you. I love you too.

She lowered her head and kissed him. He welcomed her lips and the sweet taste of her when she invited him to explore her with his tongue. They had shared intimate kisses before, and as the days continued, the contact had grown frequent enough where he was comfortable with it.

But even as comfortable as it was, his heart still hammered loudly in his chest. This was it. If he didn't ruin it, he just might get to finally make love to her.

His fingers traced the smooth skin from her hip and up to her nearest breast. Since she didn't pull away, he cupped her in the palm of his hand and groaned.

Her breasts felt even better than they looked, and he didn't think that was possible. But it was, and he couldn't wait to find out how much better things were going to get. That is, if she allowed him to continue.

He reluctantly ended the kiss and took the jar she'd been holding and returned it to the nightstand. There's no reason for that to get in the way. Too eager to care that excitement was in his voice or actions, he pulled her into his arms so he could kiss her again.

She moaned and fell into his embrace. It felt right to hold her close with her bare skin teasing him. It felt as if she belonged to him as if she had been created so that he wouldn't have to live his life alone.

His mouth left hers so he could sprinkle a trail of kisses down her neck. He was aware of many things, the feel of her back as he pressed her closer to him, the way her breasts crushed against his chest, the contented sigh drifting from her lips.

I want you, Delia, he whispered in her ear.

I want you too.

He separated from her so he could wiggle out of his pants and glanced at her when he heard her give a slight gasp. What?

Is there something wrong with me?

Well...no. But aren't you supposed to be... She motioned to his erection. —You know...

Oh. Right. Irving wasn't able to do this. As unlikely as it was that she'd believe him, he blurted out, it's a miracle! And tossed her onto her back so that he was lying on top of her.

Before she could ask any more questions, he kissed her again. All he had to do was get her back into the mood, and she'd forget all about Irving's problem.

Fortunately, she didn't take much convincing. She wrapped her legs around him and encouraged him to continue.

He didn't want to rush their first time, so he resisted the urge to enter her, though he did give into the urge to move his hips. He couldn't tell whose groans were louder, but it was apparent that she was receiving pleasure from this action just as he was.

He wanted to fully explore her, to learn all her womanly secrets, so he pulled away from her. The tip of his manhood teased him by delaying at her entrance, but he resisted the urge to rush this.

Instead, he caressed her breasts. Her nipples hardened for him, and she arched her back. His breath grew heavy at the sight. She was, without a doubt, the most desirable woman who ever lived.

Who knew lovemaking could be so incredible?

He let his hands travel down her body until his fingers reached the patch of curls that marked the entrance that held a particular interest to him.

Not that her breasts weren't exciting, in and of themselves, but the male part of him was especially drawn to this area of her body. He took his time feeling her and looking at her, growing even more aroused by her whimpers of pleasure.

He wanted to please her. For some reason that was even more important than satisfying himself, something he didn't think would be possible considering the insistent throbbing of his erection.

Giving into his curiosity, he slid his finger into her. Yes, that male part of him was going to like being in there.

She reached down and directed his movements. The fact that she took charge further motivated him to do whatever she needed to get the most enjoyment from this.

He continued until she cried out. He decided that that was the most beautiful sound he'd ever heard a woman make.

When she relaxed her hold on him, he moved over her so that he could enter her. The moment he'd been waiting for ever since he saw her coming his way in front of the courthouse was finally here, and as he slid into her, he closed his eyes and groaned.

Really, he knew it was going to be good, but he didn't know it was going to be this good.

What in the world had convinced him to wait so long? Irving should have resolved his problem weeks ago.

She wrapped her legs around his waist and allowed him to thrust deeper into her. He moved as slow as he could, knowing he could prolong the sweet agony if he did so. And he dragged it out for as long as he could before he couldn't take it anymore and had to climax.

He clenched his teeth and braced himself against the onslaught of sensation that rushed through him. Never in a million years did he imagine it'd be like this. And he thought he had a pretty good imagination.

When the last wave of pleasure failed, he collapsed on top of her, hardly aware that she was holding onto him. It took a good minute before he could think clearly.

He lifted his head so he could look at her. He brushed the stray strands of her hair from her eyes and smiled.

That was the best thing that's ever happened to me, he admitted, still breathing hard. I mean, of course, besides marrying you.

She ran her legs down his, sending a thrill through him. I want to do this again.

You won't get any complaints from me, sweetheart.

It was nice, you know. To do this and know you're not going to leave me if I get with child.

Turning serious, he inspected her and realized that it must have hurt when David ran out on her and Johnny.

No, I'm not leaving. I love you, Delia, and there's nothing that will tear us apart.

Good. Because I've grown accustomed to having you around.

You got me for keeps. Even if we have a dozen children, I'll still be here.

She balked. A dozen?

He shrugged. It's been known to happen.

Oh dear. Maybe I should rethink this being in bed with you.

Giving a playful slap on her bottom, he said, Don't you dare!

She giggled and kissed him. I wouldn't dream of it.

Content, he settled back into her arms and waited for when he had enough energy to make love to her again.

Chapter 14

Rick

Delia scanned the crowd of people the next morning. She didn't want to go into the church until she saw Sandy.

But Sandy wasn't anywhere, and that wasn't like her sister. She couldn't even focus on what her brothers were telling Owen...or what Jessica and Mary were talking about.

An uneasy feeling swelled in the pit of her stomach. Perhaps she should have run after her sister last night. But then she wouldn't have taken care of Owen and then... She blushed.

She didn't know lovemaking could involve such happiness. She glanced at him, recalling the way his hands and mouth felt on her skin.

Her body tingled from the memory. She couldn't wait to be alone with him again.

Delia ? Someone nudged her in the side.

She jumped back and cleared her throat. She realized that Mary and Jessica were staring at her. What? she asked, hoping they didn't detect what she'd been thinking about.

Sandy's here, Mary said. You wanted us to tell you if we saw her.

Delia looked in the direction Mary pointed. Oh good! Thank you. She wove through two groups until she reached her sister.

Sandy, how are you? Where's Rick and Greg?

Sandy sighed and shrugged. They're going to his parents.

You don't sound happy.

Well, I'm not. I don't feel like being here. You know how hard it is to sing hymns about loving and forgiving people when all you want to do is hit your husband over the head with a rolling pin?

I'm sorry, Sandy. Everything started out so well. I don't understand what went wrong.

What's there to understand? Rick would rather chase a squirrel than be with me.

Surely, that isn't true.

Maybe not. But it's how I feel. I could take off all my clothes and go right up to him, and he wouldn't even look up from his work.

Delia blinked. Did you try that?

Well...no.

Maybe you should.

Sandy gasped and clutched Delia's arm. Oh, I couldn't. Why not?

It's just...it's not something women do. They don't go parading in front of their husbands in broad daylight.

But you're in the privacy of your own home.

Maybe but... She let go of Delia's coat sleeve and clasped her hands together.

I'd lose the nerve.

Hasn't he seen you naked before?

Sure, he has. We've been married for a good eight years.

It's just that we're in bed.

I'm surprised at you, Sandy. You have more experience in this area than I do, but even I know that men have a hard time resisting a woman who undresses in front of them.

Really?

Try it. I guarantee that if you casually go around the room and slip off a piece of clothing here and there, you'll have his full attention.

Sandy bit her lower lip and tapped her foot on the grass.

Can something that simple work?

Oh, it can.

It worked like a charm on Owen. She grinned at the memory. She hadn't thought he'd be able to have or maintain an erection.

She didn't understand it. Maybe he was so distraught from his accident that he feared he couldn't make love. Maybe seeing a naked woman was all it took for him to forget his fears.

Well, whatever the reason, she didn't care. The point was they spent hours instead of minutes like it'd been with David enjoying each other.

Once Owen got going, there was no stopping him. She was sure that Rick would respond similarly to Sally if she stripped in front of him.

Delia winked at her sister. I bet it'll be just the thing to put the spark right back into your marriage.

Sandy seemed to consider it for a moment before nodding.

It can't hurt.

No, it can't!

Sandy finally broke into one of her familiar smiles. You're right, Delia. It just might work.

And to show you how sure I am it will, let me and Owen take Greg off your hands for the day.

Oh, there's no need for that. His parents are taking him to their house after the service. Thank you, Delia. I feel much better. Maybe now I can get through the sermon without wanting to strangle my husband.

Now Delia could get through the sermon without driving herself crazy over her sister's predicament. Giving a contented sigh, she returned to Owen.

Rick led Greg to his parents before he went to find Mr. White.

He hated it when Sandy was mad at him.

He realized his workload caused a strain in their marriage, but it didn't occur to him how upset Sandy was about it until the previous night.

Something as small as him wanting to help Irving track down a squirrel wouldn't usually upset her. She was too levelheaded for that kind of thing.

No. He knew what bothered her. It was the fact he consistently put her aside for his work that bothered her.

If there was one thing he knew, it was that marriages had to be cultivated. He'd seen enough miserable men and women come through in his line of work to see what a lack of care and attention did to a spouse.

Though divorce wasn't common back east, it happened in the west quite a bit, especially in places where the men outnumbered the women. But even if the couples didn't choose divorce, they sometimes chose to live their lives apart from each other.

He didn't want that to be the case with him and Sandy.

He found his boss staying in a group by a tree and approached him.

Mr. White, may I have a moment of your time?

The middle-aged man nodded and excused himself from his family.

Is something troubling you, Rick?

Yes. He put his hands in his pockets since he didn't know what else to do with them. Sir, I was wondering about Carl Townsend. Do you think he'll be well enough to return to work?

I don't know. Some days he feels better and other days he doesn't.

Rick feared that was the case. He glanced over his shoulder and saw that Sandy was talking to Delia. He hated knowing she was mad at him, and quite frankly, he couldn't blame her. Turning back to his boss, he said, I was wondering if you would consider hiring a third judge and hiring Jack full-time to take care of the clerical duties?

Mr. White sighed. You've been having a rough time of it for the past six months, haven't you?

The admission was hard, but he managed to say, yes, sir.

I've been wondering what to do about Carl. He's a good man. I don't want to let him go.

Of course not. Rick liked Carl and didn't want to see him go either.

But I don't want to make things harder on you than they have been. Mr. White nodded. I will hire Jack full-time, and I'll see about finding a temporary judge. It might mean a slight pay cut.

That is fine, sir. He didn't mind taking a little less home if it meant he didn't have to work overtime. Sandy, he figured, would be happy with the arrangement.

I'll get to it tomorrow morning then.

Rick breathed a sigh of relief. If he'd known, it was going to be this easy, he wouldn't have delayed the discussion for as long as he had.

Thank you, sir.

The man returned to his family, so Rick headed off to find his wife. She had just finished talking to Delia.

Sandy? he called out to her, excited that he could finally give her some good news for a change.

She stopped on her way to her parents and strode over to him.

What is it?

He took her hand and smiled at her. I just want to let you know that you're as beautiful today as the day we got married.

She frowned as if she couldn't believe her ears.

What?

I'm sorry about last night. You're right. I have been working too hard. I just talked to Mr. White, and he said he'd hire a temporary judge and let Jack work full-time.

Her eyes lit up and she squeezed his hand.

Really, Rick?

It'll mean a cut in my pay, he warned her.

Oh. Well, how much of a cut?

He raised an eyebrow at her.

And I thought you cared more about me than the money.

She giggled and patted his arm.

Oh, I was teasing, and you know it.

He let go of her hand so he could slip his arm around her waist and pull her closer. I have missed being with you.

Rick, she whispered, glancing around, you shouldn't be holding me this close in public.

A sly grin crossed his face as he leaned forward and whispered.

This is nothing, honey. Just wait until we get home.

My parents agreed to take care of Greg until six.

She blushed but her eyes twinkled with excitement.

I have a surprise for you.

Really? What is it?

You'll have to wait and see. She gave him a quick kiss on the cheek.

I can't wait, he told her, enjoying the anticipation, even as it was killing him. Knowing Sandy, it was going to be worth the wait. His body was already anxious to be alone with her. It'd been much too long since they had time to be together for a decent amount of time.

I love you.

I love you too, Rick.

Glad that things were no longer tense between them, he led her into the church when it was time for the service to begin.

Owen pounded the last board onto the attic floor and tested it to make sure it was in place. Good. Setting down the hammer, he stood up and walked over the new section of flooring. It wasn't perfect, but it worked. No one else would be falling through the floor.

Satisfied, he went over to the board he had set over the hole in the side of the wall. It was a temporary fix. He needed to take care of the outside of the house. But that would have to be on a day when he didn't have work. As it was, he was going to be late if he didn't get a move on.

He collected the rest of the boards, the hammer and box of nails and carefully went down the ladder.

Once he put everything away in the little shed out back, he found Delia sitting in the parlor making a dress for one of the women in town.

Johnny was outside playing with what little snow covering the ground. She looked out the window and watched him.

Since they had a moment of privacy, Owen hurried over to her and gave her a big hug.

She shrieked and then laughed.

You scared me. Setting her things aside, she hugged him back.

Did you secure the attic?

I did. He kissed her neck.

She giggled and ran her hands down his back.

So, no more squirrels will get into the house?

Not unless you want them to.

Wrapping her legs around his waist, she brought him closer to her.

He groaned. I must go to work.

Just giving you an idea of what'll happen tonight.

Giving her a long kiss, he caressed her breasts. Reluctant, he pulled away from her. I can't wait.

Me neither.

She squeezed his bottom.

You don't play fair, honey. He removed himself from the tempting position so he could sit next to her. He took her hands in his and debated, once again, if he should tell her the truth.

She snuggled against him and smiled. I thought you had to go to work.

I do. But I thought I should tell you something first.

What is it?

He hesitated. Could he do this? Would she still love him if she knew he lied to her...to everyone? He examined her eyes. What if she didn't love him once she knew he wasn't the invincible Irving Spencer? He released his breath. It was wrong to withhold the truth. He knew it was. But he couldn't bring himself to tell her.

Not today.

Maybe tomorrow.

Maybe next week.

He just needed time to think of the right words. Then he'd tell her in a way that would ease the shock, and she'd understand why he did the things he did. Yes. He'd figure out what to say first.

After he gave her another kiss, he asked, Will you make a pie?

She laughed and nudged him in the side. You sure did look serious for someone who wanted something simple. Yes. I'll make you a pie.

She kissed him on the cheek.

Thanks, Delia. He grinned and kissed her back.

Standing, he took a deep breath and patted his vest. Once he slipped his badge on, he'd be in proper attire.

I should be back around eight.

I can't wait, she replied, winking.

Neither could he. He recalled how her body felt under his. The male part of him did as well since it made no fuss to remind him of how eager it was to spend time alone with her.

He sighed and retrieved his coat. Glancing back at her, he hoped that bedtime would come very soon. If Sheriff Meyer kept him busy enough, the time would go fast. Hopefully, it would be a busy day.

Once he had his coat on, he put on his hat and left the house. He saw Johnny rolling a snowball across the lawn, picking up fragments of the snow as he went along.

How are you doing, squirt?

Owen called out as he fastened the top buttons of his coat.

I'm making a big ball! Johnny replied.

You know, where I grew up, we only had snow once, and as soon as the flakes touched the ground, they melted.

Johnny stopped rolling his ball and frowned at him.

That's not fun.

But I could fish this time of year without having to wear a coat.

He shrugged. I can do that when it gets warm.

He had to admire the kid's logic.

True. Maybe being in Nebraska is better than being down south. He didn't miss being in Louisiana. Not with Delia and Johnny right here. But sometimes, he did wonder how his aunt was doing.

He prayed Big Roy never figured out that she had the money. If he believed Owen deposited the cash into the bank, then she was safe.

He adjusted his collar to brace against the chill in the air and waved at the youngster. I'll see you when I get back. Be sure to take care of your ma while I'm gone.

The boy nodded, but he'd already turned his attention back to his snowball.

A grin on Owen's face, he went to get the horse ready for the ride into town.

CHAPTER 15

Owen the Deputy

Owen patted his stomach and leaned back in the chair at the sheriff's desk. If he had to eat another bite of anything, he was going to burst. Those Larson women knew how to stuff a man senseless. Who knew Thanksgiving could render a man tired for days on end?

He sat up straight. He couldn't even take a deep breath.

To finish up the leftovers, Delia persuaded him to have an extra helping of thanksgiving breakfast that morning.

He hoped that they were officially done. He'd had enough of turkey to last a lifetime. Now it was time for his poor stomach to get a break.

He picked up the latest papers on Meyer's desk and sorted through them. Good. None were of him. But there was one on Robert Scott. Owen frowned. Why did the name Robert sound familiar? Oh yes. He was the name Joshua had written and placed in his wallet when Owen went to Guy Ike's house.

That was the day of the shoot-out. He shivered at the memory. He hoped shoot-outs didn't happen often in Omaha.

He looked back at the paper and read the caption under the rough sketch of the bearded man. Kidnapping children.

Owen's jaw clenched. What in the world would a man do that for? He thought of Johnny. If someone kidnapped him...

For once, Owen was glad he was a deputy. At least he had some leads that another father didn't.

He studied Robert's face. If he came across this man, he'd get him, even if he had to use a dozen fishing rods...or try his hand at the gun in his holster.

But what if Robert isn't guilty? What if he was framed for something to cover up for someone else?

Owen sat back for a moment and considered the implications. How many men were falsely accused of something and put on a Wanted poster? Probably most of those men were guilty.

But how could, one be sure? Still, Robert had a connection to Guy and Jimmy.

But I have a connection to Big Roy.

He looked back at Robert's picture. Innocent until proven guilty. If I do find you, I'll make sure that this is accurate. And if it is...

Well, if it was, then all bets were off, and he'd do his part to make sure justice was served.

The door opened and someone asked, is Sheriff Meyer here?

Owen stilled. He didn't look up from the paper right away. He didn't have to because he recognized that low rumble.

He winced and set the paper down. So, this was it. The moment he'd dreaded ever since he married Delia.

Steeling his resolve, he dared to look in Irving Spencer's direction. The blood drained from Owen's face. The man was larger than he remembered. Irving Spencer wasn't six or six-and a-half feet tall. This monster was seven feet! And Owen barely made it to five-eight.

The man was also built like a brick wall. He's going to kill me! It'd be an easy thing for him to do too.

All Irving needed to do was pound him once on the head and into the ground he'd go. Irving didn't even need to dig a hole first.

Well, Owen gulped, at least I had my last meal.

Irving narrowed his eyes at him. His bushy black eyebrows formed a perfect V. You look familiar. Do I know you?

No, Owen squeaked. He cleared his throat and tried to say, no again, but he only squeaked a higher note.

Oh wait. I remember you. You were in the forest in Tennessee. That's where I found Big Roy. Then Irving gave him a huge smile and balled his fists. He underestimated me.

Owen gulped. How anyone could underestimate this monster of a man bewildered him. Surely, Irving realized that too.

No matter. He won't be causing trouble anymore.

Really? That meant his aunt was safe!

Irving's eyes fell to Owen's badge. I see Meyer found another deputy.

Not exactly. And Irving wasn't going to be happy at all when he discovered who had the job.

The door opened again and this time the sheriff walked in.

Of course. It would have to be Sheriff Meyer! Owen thought.

Why would it be otherwise? His luck had just taken a nosedive. Well, except for finding out Big Roy was no longer a problem. That was good. Probably the only good thing right now.

The sheriff looked up at the real Irving. Howdy. How can I help you?

You must be Meyer. Irving motioned to the man's badge.

That's right. Do you need help with something?

I came to be your deputy, but I see you already got one.

Yep. Sure do. Sheriff Meyer nodded and adjusted his hat. Irving Spencer is the best there is.

Owen cringed. Oh great. So much for hoping Irving would quietly slip out of town. For a split second there, he had this wonderful fantasy where Irving would find out there was a deputy, thank the sheriff and leave...never to be seen or heard from again. But Meyer had to indicate that Owen was Irving Spencer and now the cat was out of the bag. And that meant Owen was in deep trouble.

As predicted, Irving turned his steel cold eyes in Owen's direction. What's your name?

Owen moved his mouth, but no answer came out of it...unless one counted a whimper an actual reply.

He's Irving Spencer, Sheriff Meyer said.

Owen sunk further into the chair. This was not good.

Oh, there was absolutely no way this could end well.

He can't be Irving Spencer, the mammoth of a man said. I'm Irving Spencer.

Then there must be two Irvings. The sheriff shrugged.

This one came from South Carolina to work for me.

I'm from South Carolina.

The sheriff frowned. And he married Delia Larson, he slowly added.

I'm supposed to marry Delia Larson. Because of the boy. Johnny.

Owen suddenly noticed how hot it was in the place. He glanced around the jailhouse and saw no means of escape. His exit was blocked by Meyer and Spencer who looked at each other, and then, in perfect unison, turned their gazes to Owen.

Well, Owen had only one recourse before the law came crashing down on him.

He jumped over the desk and hightailed it right into the cell. He slammed the door and tested it. Good. Irving couldn't come after him. Not when Owen had the key in his pocket!

He might be in jail, but at least he'd just preserved his life. He backed up until his legs hit the cot. He fell on it.

The two men crept forward; their eyes narrowed at him as if they were stalking a rodent.

Owen cleared his throat and gave a weak chuckle. Look, it's all simple when you think about it. You see, Big Roy came after me, so I ran.

He motioned to Irving. He saw Big Roy in Tennessee. Well, Big Roy was chasing me because I won some money from him at the saloon. Um... He cleared his throat and leapt up on the bed so he could scurry further away from the men who stepped closer to the bars.

Oh goodness, those bars would hold them back, right? I borrowed Irving's horse and clothes so I could get away.

You have my horse? Irving demanded, crossing his arms, and shooting him the evil eye or at least that's how Owen interpreted the keen stare.

Owen tried to laugh but it came out sounding like another pathetic whimper. It sort of...left...when I got on a train Hmmm....

Irving didn't stop staring at him.

So, I...uh...came here. I was just going to get a haircut, shave and eat. Then I was going to be out of here. But... His gaze shifted to the sheriff who shook his head in disappointment.

But then the sheriff saw your hat and thought I was you.

Then, the next thing I know, I'm getting married. He let out another weak chuckle. Funny, huh?

I'm not laughing, Irving said, his face unreadable.

Neither am I, the sheriff added.

Owen gave up and cried out, please, don't hang me! I didn't mean to kill Michael!

Irving's eyes grew wide, and he snapped his fingers.

That's where I've seen you. You're wanted for murder!

It was an accident! I didn't mean to kill him! Big Roy sent him after me. He had a knife. I had no choice!

You're in a lot of trouble, son, the sheriff said. And it isn't just Michael.

You stole a horse. You came here and impersonated a deputy. You married a woman that belonged to another man, and you spent all these months lying to all of us.

What you need is a lawyer. He held out his hand. Give me the badge and key.

Owen didn't know why but the command hurt.

He knew he couldn't be the deputy anymore, and yet, he wished he could.

Trying not to show how this affected him, he slowly stepped down from the cot. He dug his hand into his pocket and pulled out the key.

Then he removed the badge. His hands trembled as he handed them over.

The sheriff took them but wouldn't look him in the eye.

Instead, he handed them to Irving. Let's see what we can do about getting this mess straightened out.

Mess? Owen grabbed the bars. Wait! You don't mean Delia, do you?

They didn't answer.

He watched them leave the jailhouse and fought the urge to cry. He deserved what he was getting. He knew what he was doing was wrong, but he'd done it anyway. And who knew if Delia would want to stay with him when she found out the truth?

What a way to find out! And from the real Irving himself.

Owen's shoulders slumped as he made his way back to the cot. He should have told her. At least, if she already knew, then she'd be prepared for it. No. It was best she didn't know.

Now, they couldn't arrest her for aiding a Wanted man. She was innocent, and that made her safe. He put his face in his hands.

Would she want to stay married to him? He'd already lost his job, his reputation, and his freedom. That was manageable if she was with him. But if she wasn't... If Jeremy wasn't...

He closed his eyes and tried not to think about it.

Delia grabbed her broom. Stay here, she told Johnny who was eating at the kitchen table.

She looked back out the window. She didn't know whether to be angry or afraid. Why was David coming out to see her? Was it because Owen arrested him?

Glancing over her shoulder to make sure her son was still at the table, she put her coat on and stormed onto the porch.

He got off his horse. When he looked in her direction, he didn't seem concerned by the fact that she was ready to whack him with the broom if he got too close.

Hi there, Delia.

Get away from here, she snapped.

He walked over to the bottom step of the porch and stopped just two inches shy of her being able to hit him with the broom.

Placing his hands on his hips, he tilted his head up so he could make eye contact.

I want my son.

He's not your son. She tightened her grip on the broom handle and got ready to strike if needed.

That's not what you told me five years ago.

She gritted her teeth. Irving Spencer is his pa now.

He smirked at her and adjusted his suspenders. That's just it, ain't it? The real Irving Spencer just got into town today.

Get out of here!

You think I'm making this up?

Since when did you tell me the truth about anything?

Oh Delia, I love you. I want to marry you. It's just this one time. We're engaged anyway.' You make me want to throw up.

And that much was the truth. Her stomach was rumbling like crazy at the sight of him. She swallowed the bile in her throat.

She tried to hit him with the broom, but she hit dead air.

You can go on down to the jailhouse and check for yourself if you'd like, David said, seeming to be unconcerned that he'd come close to being knocked over. You should see him, Delia. He's huge. He makes that Owen Russell you married look like a pipsqueak.

She blinked through the ringing in her ears.

What name did you say?

He threw his head back and laughed. Sound familiar? I thought so too. Owen Russell is on the run, sweetheart. He's a wanted man, and he came here posing as Irving Spencer.

No. It couldn't be true. She shook her head and tried to focus through the tumult in her stomach. Owen wouldn't lie to her like that. Owen? Owen! What were the chances Irving Spencer would have that nickname?

Another rush of bile came up her throat. Oh no. She just knew she was going to throw up!

David grinned. Poor Delia. Well, it was worth a shot, I guess. Can't blame this one on you.

He got up on the first step.

She hit him across the head with the broom. You're not getting near my son!

He rubbed the side of his head and glared at her. You have no right to keep me away from him!

Owen Russell is still married to me. And he's Johnny's pa, even if he is a wanted man! Her stomach tossed. A wanted man? Oh, she was going to vomit for sure!

Don't make this difficult, Delia, David said, his expression darkening. I told you I'd do right by you and marry you.

And I told you no! She whacked him again, sending him through the air.

He landed on his back and groaned.

Get off my property! she screamed, shaking. Leave me and my son alone! She ran down the steps and got ready to whack him again.

He quickly got up and ran from her.

She chased him, holding her broom over her head.

Hopping up on his horse, he said, I'll get my son next time I come out here, Delia!

You'll get Johnny over my dead body.

Then she whacked the horse which bucked back, nearly knocking David off.

Unfortunately, David managed to stay on the animal.

He's my son too. Then, before she could swing the broom again, he kicked the horse in the sides and bolted off the property.

Even though she was still trembling, she lowered the broom and began to cry. No. It couldn't be true! He couldn't take Johnny from her. He was just lying. That's what he did best.

From the moment she met him, he told her things that didn't come to pass.

And now she just learned that her husband was the same way. No. Owen wouldn't do that. He wouldn't do that! What man would lie to a woman so he could marry her and be a father to a child that wasn't his?

"I'd like you to call me Owen."

"Why Owen?" she asked him. "I'd think your nickname would be something like Irv."

"My aunt called me Owen. But I'd rather you call me that when it's just us."

She didn't know whether to keep crying or throw up. So, at the end, she did both.

She remained kneeling in the snow, aware that it was cold and wet but not truly feeling it.

Why her? Of all the women out there, why did she have the uncanny ability to attract the wrong men? Was there a dark cloud hanging over the house when she was born or something?

How could Owen do this to her? She thought she knew him. She thought it was odd that he went by Owen but figured that some people had nicknames that had nothing to do with their real names.

She was a horrible judge of character. She really had no common sense when it came to men.

Ma?

Blinking through her tears, she looked over her shoulder and saw her son watching her from the porch. She struggled to her feet and went over to him. Pulling him into her arms, she swore she would do whatever it took to keep Johnny safe with her.

It didn't matter what else happened to her. If staying married to a man who was wanted by the law was the only way she could keep him, she would. It wasn't that Owen was a bad man. He was always good to Johnny. But what had he done? She didn't understand it.

So many emotions were whirling inside of her, and she didn't know what to do. One minute she wanted to smack Owen and the next she wanted to go to him and ask him to explain what was going on.

I'll find Sandy. Rick is a judge. Surely, he'll have some ideas.

Already feeling better, she turned Johnny to the open doorway. Get your coat and boots on, sweetie. We're going to see your aunt and uncle.

Which ones?

Sandy and Rick. She was still trembling, but she set the broom down and went into the house to get his coat.

They'll know what to do.

Though she spoke aloud, she wasn't directing the last statement to him. It was so unreal. Like being stuck in a dream. Parts of it made sense, but most of it didn't.

She wiped her wet cheeks on her coat sleeve and placed a hat on her head. It wasn't hopeless. Whenever things looked hopeless in the past, she managed through it.

She remembered how horrible things seemed when she told her parents she was pregnant.

David had just left town, leaving her all alone to figure things out. And she got through that. If she could handle that, she could handle this too. She just needed to think.

Nothing was hopeless as long as she kept going.

Always look forward. Never look back.

She turned to Johnny who finished putting his last boot on. Good. He was ready. Let's go. She put her arm around his shoulders and directed him out of the house.

As she closed the door, Johnny said, There's Aunt Sandy.

She looked over in the direction he pointed to. Yes.

There was Aunt Sandy alright. And Aunt Sandy brought Mary and their children Greg and Isaac.

Delia 's heart plummeted. If Sandy brought Mary out, then there was no doubt that what David said was true.

Sandy knew that Mary would be a source of comfort to Delia. Mary would be the one to break the news to her because Mary somehow knew the right words to say, no matter how bleak the situation.

Well, even if they came to tell her that Owen was not really Irving Spencer, Delia still needed to get things straightened out.

As she and Johnny walked down the first step of the porch, she caught sight of four horses. She frowned. Her brothers knew too? This wasn't going to be fun. For any of them.

Taking her son's hand, she stabilized her nerves and headed down the rest of the steps.

CHAPTER 16

Owen is Locked up

Owen jumped up as soon as the door to the jailhouse opened. He rushed over to the bars to see if Delia had come. She did. But she also brought Sandy and her four brothers with her.

Four very angry looking brothers. He immediately stepped back as the four intense men surrounded the cell. He examined the bars. He hoped the steel was strong enough to keep them out.

They looked like they were ready to rip him apart and feed his remains to the vultures.

You're lucky you're in there! Tom yelled, pointing an accusing finger at him. Because if you weren't, we'd run you out of town.

How could you do this to our sister? Richard demanded, shaking the bars.

Owen swallowed the lump in his throat and backed up until he hit the wall.

He glanced at the small window and wondered if he could escape if he squeezed through it. No. That was ridiculous. He was much safer here with the bars protecting him than in the open where these men could chase him down.

First David and now him, Stevie said in disgust. Is there no end to what Delia must go through?

Why did you do it? Sandy asked. She left Delia in the corner of the room and stormed up to the bars. Well? Why did you do it?

You knew you weren't Irving, Stevie agreed.

Owen thought of how to respond. Really was there anything he could possibly say that would ward off the evil vibes coming his way?

Richard shook the bars again. Answer her!

His voice squeaked so he loosened his collar and cleared his throat. It may have been snowing outside, but it was incredibly hot here. Sweat was literally dripping down his back.

Well. He glanced at Delia who just stood to the side of the room and stared at him. He couldn't figure out what she was thinking. Horrified... stunned...appalled... Probably that and more.

What were you thinking? Richard screamed.

Owen jerked and directed his attention to five irate people.

Shrugging, he managed out a weak, I saw her, and she was so beautiful.

The group groaned and rolled their eyes.

That's just what I thought, Richard said, shaking his head. He wasn't thinking. Not with his brain anyway. This is just great, Stevie muttered.

Looking at his brothers, he asked, what are we supposed to do with him?

Joel sighed. There's nothing we can do. He's well protected in there.

Richard banged the bars. How long were you going to let this go on? Were you ever going to tell us the truth? He pointed to Delia.

Were you ever going to tell her?

Owen shifted from one foot to the other, aware that there wasn't anything he could say to alleviate their anger.

I'm sorry. I didn't want to lie to everyone. By the looks on their faces, it was clear they didn't believe him. And who could blame them?

It's just that... Owen rubbed the back of his neck. Yep.

It was hotter than the dog days of August in this place.

Clearing his throat again, he said, down in Louisiana, my uncle gambled away all his money and then killed himself. My aunt had nothing to her name, and they were ready to take her home, so I went to the saloon.

Sandy gasped and brought her hand to her mouth.

I didn't do that, he quickly assured her. I went to get the money back. I got lucky and won the money back after a full night of playing poker. Big Roy and his men didn't take too well to that. They found me a couple of days later and tried to kill me.

I managed to get out of Louisiana.

So how does this involve Irving Spencer? Richard asked.

I ran into him while I was on the run. Big Roy found me in a wooded area and was chasing me. I stumbled upon Irving's campsite by mistake and took his clothes while he was, he glanced at Sandy and Delia answering nature's call.

What did you need his clothes for?

I was naked.

What were you doing in the forest without any clothes on? Richard angrily asked.

Taking a swim in the river. I wanted to get clean. Big Roy found my horse before I had a chance to get back into my clothes.

So, when I found a pile of clean clothes at least I assume they were clean, I put them on. By the time Big Roy came up to the campsite, I was on Irving's horse and got out of there.

I don't feel good, Delia said, clutching her stomach.

Sandy ran over to her and put an arm around her shoulders.

Shooting a scolding look at Owen, she asked, Are you happy?

Look at what you're doing to her!

Delia sat on the bench and Sandy sat beside her, still hugging her sister.

Owen shuddered. I'm so sorry, Delia. I never meant to hurt you.

You'll answer our questions right now! Tom interrupted.

Owen quieted and waited.

Tom nudged Richard in the side. Go on.

Richard nodded. So, you ended up in Omaha and decided to be Irving?

No. Well, I mean it turned out that way, Owen began, but that wasn't what I originally intended. I was just passing through. I saw the Wanted posters.

Big Roy framed me for murder, but I didn't mean to kill Michael.

Delia groaned. I think I'm going to throw up.

You murdered someone! Stevie shouted, his eyes nearly popping out of his head.

Owen threw his hands up in the air, as he'd seen other outlaws do when they were caught. He was going to kill me! I had to protect myself.

Then why was your face on a Wanted poster?

I don't know. I think Big Roy told the local sheriff that I killed Michael on purpose.

The sound of Delia throwing up into the trashcan Sandy held for her stopped the interrogation. The five men winced, and Owen had to look away in case he joined her.

Once the horrible sound stopped, his stomach settled.

Sandy marched over to the cell and showed him the trashcan. I ought to fling this in there for what you did to her!

Now, Sandy, Richard began, let's not be gross.

She grunted. I've never seen Dela this upset. She turned to Owen. I hope you're happy. I just hope you're happy with what you're putting her through!

Owen hastened to a free section of the bars so he could see his wife. He winced. She was too pale. This wasn't good.

Delia, I love you. I only said I was Irving because the sheriff came up to me and I thought he was going to hang me.

Then I married you, and I think you're the most wonderful woman a man could ever have. Get away from her!

Richard ran over to him. Owen immediately hurried back to the safe area of his cell where no one could touch him. He tried to look around Richard to see if Delia might give him some leeway, but Richard expertly shifted so his view of her was blocked.

Richard pointed at him. You're not having anything to do with Delia ever again. Do you understand? You're a wanted man. You can stand trial before a judge, and maybe he'll release you.

But there's no way you'll ever get near our sister again. Tom nodded his agreement. We'll chase you out of town if we must. We won't have anyone else hurting her.

The door opened and the infamous Irving Spencer entered the building with the sheriff close behind.

Owen pressed his back to the wall. He was still overwhelmed by the sheer brute strength of the formidable tower of a man. As if the brothers secretly felt the same way, they cowered in his presence.

Owen had no doubt that if the roles were reversed if he was built like Irving that the brothers would think twice before gaining up on him. Irving could take on an entire town and still be left standing.

I need to speak to the prisoner, Irving said in a low, controlled voice.

Without question or even a hint of hesitation the brothers took Sandy and Delia out of the jailhouse.

Owen rolled his eyes. Yep, it was too bad he wasn't actually built like Irving. The man didn't even has to raise his voice to get four tough brothers to run off like a bunch of women.

Irving was the perfect man, and Owen was really beginning to resent that. Didn't the man has one flaw?

Irving took the key out of his pocket and opened the cell door.

Startled, Owen braced himself against the wall and glanced at the window. Why did it have to be so small? There was no escaping this beast! He shot an anxious look at the sheriff who simply sighed, shook his head, and went to his desk. Oh great.

Sheriff Meyer was going to leave him alone in the cell with Irving the Monster Spencer. And Irving couldn't be happy with him since he took his job and Delia from him.

To Owen's surprise, Irving sat on the cot and calmly folded his arms. What do you know about Big Roy?

Of all the things Owen expected, this wasn't on the list.

W-what?

You had personal dealings with Big Roy. He's a sneaky fox. Escaped prison. Though he wouldn't has if I'd been there.

He slammed his fist into the palm of his hand. Now the weasel's hiding.

Owen winced.

He directed his confident gaze to Owen. The problem is, I need something to lure him out from his hiding spot.

It took a moment before Irving's meaning dawned on Owen. Gasping, Owen tapped his chest.

Me? I'm bait?

Don't think of it as being bait. Think of it as giving a helping hand. You know all about taking care of the scum. You did become me.

He gulped but nodded.

And in return for your help, I will talk to the judge about going easy on you.

Owen wiped his sweaty hands on his pants. What about Delia?

What about her?

Well...I married her, you know?

He nodded.

I want to stay married to her. That is, if she'd still want to be married to him Owen Russell. He scanned Irving. Did he even stand a chance against Irving?

I only agreed to marry her to help her out. David Jenkins runs around with a suspicious crowd.

Really? What did he do?

Nothing...yet. His name popped up awhile back though.

Seems suspicious when a thief makes a comment. Slip of the tongue or intentional, I don't know. But either way, I got to figure him out too.

He stood up and placed his hands on his hips. His legs were spread apart, and he stared Owen down as if he were bracing for a fight.

What'd you say?

Adjusting his collar again, Owen asked, I get to stay with Delia then?

If she'll, have you. She didn't look so happy just now.

True. And she had every right to be mad. But she loved him. No. Not exactly. She loved him as Irving Spencer. Still, he had been his true self around her. He might have assumed a different name and a deputy job, but he'd been who he really was with her.

Surely, she'd remember that. When they were alone, it wasn't possible to hide who he really was. He just hoped she really would remember that. He couldn't imagine his life without her or Johnny. Even if she had four brothers ready to take off his head.

Well, he had to try. He nodded. I'll help you get Big Roy. Good. The matter done, Irving headed out of the cell and locked the door.

Relieved he was still in one piece, Owen relaxed and exhaled.

CHAPTER 17

Owen Russell

Delia didn't feel like dealing with anyone now. Her mind was a jumble of thoughts, and her relatives weren't helping.

Her brothers and Sandy sat around the kitchen table trying to decide what to do about the situation while Greg, Johnny, and Isaac played with the dog in the backyard.

Mary stayed out there to watch them from where she sat in the chair next to the house.

Maybe Delia shouldn't have come to Sandy's house after they left the jail. Maybe she should have just gone home. She watched the children as they laughed and took turns throwing the ball for the dog to catch. It was simple for them.

Children didn't sit and analyze things. They either liked something or they didn't, and they acted accordingly.

Taking a deep breath, she closed her eyes and rested her forehead against the cool glass of the window. Her hand fell to her abdomen. She should've realized it sooner, but she and Owen had stayed up well into the night to enjoy lovemaking.

The fatigue was easy to explain. Today when she found out that he was really Owen Russell, instead of Irving, Owen. Spencer Naturally, it made her sick to her stomach.

It wasn't until she was at the jail and throwing up into the trashcan that she realized what was going on. She hadn't thrown up since she was carrying Johnny.

I found something we can use, Rick said as he entered the kitchen.

Startled that he was in the room, Delia's eyes flew open as she turned from the window.

I hope it's good, Richard replied, looking sour.

All Delia must do is get an annulment; Rick told the group. He didn't even seem to notice that she was right there in the corner of the room, for he kept his gaze on the group crowded around the table.

Delia didn't know she was marrying Owen Russell. She thought she was marrying Irving Spencer.

Therefore, the marriage is null and void. Even though he signed the license with his real name? Richard asked.

She didn't know he did that. None of us did.

You're a judge, Rick. Why didn't you double check?

Sandy stood up and went to her husband's side. Why didn't any of us think to double check? Were we supposed to know that Owen was an imposter?

I'll check the names on all marriage licenses in the future and make sure no one leaves blotches of ink on their names, Rick said. I can't do anything about the past. But Sandy's right.

It didn't occur to me that Owen was lying.

Stevie sighed and set down the coffee cup. None of us would have thought someone would do something that underhanded.

Richard groaned. Fine. What's done is done. We need to figure out what to do now. Are you sure Jenny can get an annulment?

Yes, Rick said. Here's the law. He handed Richard the piece of paper.

After Richard read it, he nodded and handed it to Tom.

Good. Then let's get this annulment over with.

Delia stepped forward and yelled over their chorus of agreement. —Isn't anyone going to ask me what I plan to do Tom glanced at her. It's obvious. Owen is scum.

You're getting rid of bad rubbish.

The others nodded.

No, she argued, crossing her arms. I am not getting an annulment.

They gasped with apparent shock.

The room was so quiet that Delia swore she could hear a needle bounce off the floor. I'm expecting his child, she finally said. I'm staying married to him.

Richard threw his hands up in the air. How is it possible that you keep getting pregnant by the wrong men?

Her face flushed with anger. Excuse me?

First David and now Owen.

For your information, I was married to Owen. It was perfectly alright for me to be intimate with him!

Sandy shook her head. I thought that wasn't possible.

It wasn't possible with Irving Spencer, she told her sister, knowing that only Sally knew of Irving's impotence.

A flicker of understanding lit Sally's eyes. Oh. Then she blinked and shook her head again.

But didn't it dawn on you that you married the wrong man since Owen could... She glanced at their attentive audience before directing her gaze back to Delia.

Well...you know.

For a moment but then I assumed whatever caused the problem corrected itself.

Problem? Tom asked. What problem?

Stevie rolled his eyes. You really have no idea what they're talking about?

Joel snorted. I'm younger than you, and even I know what Sandy means. Boy, Tom. You sure are dumb.

Tom glared at his brothers.

Richard grimaced and stood up. I don't care what the details are.

Delia, you can't stay with him. He lied to you to all of us and he killed someone.

To defend himself, Delia pointed out.

That hasn't been proven, Richard said.

And it hasn't been not proven. She groaned. Aren't we all innocent until proven guilty?

Oh sure. We made that mistake when you married him.

We're not going to fall for that again.

Delia had had enough. She headed for the kitchen door.

Where are you going? Sandy asked.

I need to think things over without the lot of you telling me what to do, she snapped as she flung the door open.

In case you haven't noticed, I'm an adult woman. I'm perfectly capable of deciding what's best for me and my children.

Before anyone could protest, she stepped outside and slammed the door.

Mary jerked and turned to Delia. She pressed a hand to her heart and smiled.

You gave me a good scare.

Johnny ran over to Delia. Is Pa here yet?

Delia smiled as she stroked his cheek. Not yet, honey. I need to talk to your Aunt Mary. Will you be a good boy for me and play with your cousins?

Though he looked disappointed, he nodded and went back to the two boys who were petting a very happy dog.

Delia pulled the other remaining chair in the yard so that it was next to Mary's and sat down.

At a time like this, she needed someone with a level head who could do more listening than talking. Mary, I don't know what to do. I mean, I know what Owen did was wrong, but who can really blame him? He expected to be hung. If I were in his situation, I'd probably do the same thing.

Mary nodded.

You weren't here when I was with David, Delia continued. I thought we were going to get married, and when I told him I was with child, he said we'd have to marry sooner than planned.

Well, the next thing I knew, he bolted out of town. His mother wouldn't even have anything to do with me. She blamed me for making him leave. Can you believe that? I didn't get myself in the family way. Sure, I had a part, but I wasn't in it alone.

Anyway, my brothers were so mad they searched all over for David but couldn't find him.

They insisted I stay home after Johnny was born, but I was tired of them telling me what to do.

So, when I found the boarding house and worked out an agreement with the landlady to make my rent less, I moved out.

And now they want to tell me what to do about Owen.

Maybe I'm wrong for wanting to stay with him, but I think that's what I want to do.

I don't know exactly what happened to land him here, but he showed up when I needed someone to marry.

I don't think the timing was a coincidence. I think I was meant to be with him. And I can't imagine that with all the time I spent with him, he was pretending to be someone he's not.

No one can put on that good of a show. You get to learn about people when you live with them. You know what I mean?

Mary smiled and nodded. Yes, I know.

Delia already felt better. It was nice to finally speak her thoughts. She released her breath and relaxed.

You know what Owen told me while my brothers were harassing him? He said I was the most wonderful woman a man could have. No one, not even David when he was sweet talking me so he could sleep with me, ever said that to me before.

That's how he treats me too.

And even though they don't like it, I love him.

I don't think they are opposed to you loving Owen, Mary said. They're worried you'll get hurt again. But then, doesn't every marriage suffer its trials? We all get hurt at some point, whether the other person intended to hurt us or not. As long as there are imperfect people, there will be problems.

I think I should take you in there so you can explain that to them.

Oh no. I wouldn't go near them right now. They're too hot-headed. Once they calm down enough to think straight, I can give my spiel.

Delia laughed. They can get so irrational at times, can't they?

She chuckled. They have their moments. As much as I adore your family, I've learned that there are times to stick with the children.

Smart idea. No wonder Stevie enjoys being with you.

She took a deep breath. I need to see Owen if the sheriff will let me.

I think everything will work out. Owen seems like a good man who just got stuck in a bad situation.

I think that too. Thank you, Mary. It's no wonder you're my dearest friend.

You're mine too, Delia.

Already feeling much better, Delia stood up and called Johnny who came over to her. We're going to see your pa.

The boy's eyes lit up. There was no denying the attachment he shared with Owen, and Owen was just as attached to him.

Taking his hand in hers, she said good-bye to Mary and the boys and quickly snuck out of the yard with her son. She figured that she didn't have to literally run, but she wasn't sure if they would discover where she went. If they did, there was no doubt they'd drag her back. She knew Mary would stall them for a while.

Sooner or later though, they were bound to track her down. By the time they reached the jailhouse, Irving opened the door. She gave a slight gasp and stepped back. True, she'd seen him already, but he hadn't been standing right in front of her.

He was enormous. No wonder criminals shook in their boots when they knew he was coming.

Good afternoon, Delia, Irving calmly said.

She cleared her throat and nervously replied, Hello, Irving. Uh... Can I see Owen?

He furrowed his eyebrows. Are you sure?

I want to see my pa! Johnny insisted.

Honey, shhh. She turned from her son and looked back at Irving.

Yes. I wish to talk to him. Is that alright?

He shrugged. It's fine with me if you don't run off with him.

She furrowed her eyebrows. Just what did he mean by that?

He gave a slight smile. I meant I didn't want the prisoner to escape.

She relaxed. Oh. I thought you meant... She had thought he meant that he didn't want her to stay married to Owen. But he hadn't, and she didn't want to explain it.

Looking at Irving, she knew that they wouldn't have made a good match.

She would have married him for her son, but he wouldn't have been her first choice.

She glanced inside the jailhouse. There, in the cell, sat the man she would have chosen. Returning her gaze to Irving, she asked.

So, I can talk to him?

Follow me. He led her into the building. Meyer, I got the wife wanting to see her husband.

Johnny broke free from her and ran over to the cell, calling out Pa!

Owen's face lit up and he eagerly ran over to the bars so he could hug Jeremy... Well, as much as he could with the bars between them.

The tender moment brought tears to Jenny's eyes. How many times had she seen fathers and their sons and wished Johnny could have a pa that loved him too? Wiping her eyes, she turned to the sheriff and deputy.

Can we go into the cell? You can lock us all in if you want. That might offer a forte of protection too, in case her brothers came to get her and Johnny.

The sheriff nodded. I see no harm in that.

Irving led her to the cell and opened it so she and Johnny could be with Owen.

As he locked the door, he said, Let the sheriff know when you're ready to leave. I have some investigating to do around town.

When he turned to leave, Owen ran over to her and hugged her. Oh Delia. Thank you for coming back.

She held onto him, taking comfort in his embrace.

Owen, is there anything else you didn't tell me?

She had to know. If she was going to stay married to him, she had to know everything. Then they could start with a clean slate.

Pa? Johnny tugged on his pants.

He pulled away from her so he could pick Johnny up. I grew up in Baton Rouge, Louisiana. I had an uneventful childhood.

My pa was a fisherman, so when I grew up, that's what I became. I'm not a deputy, as you already know. I fish and then sell whatever I catch. My parents passed on early in my life.

First my mother. Then my father. I went to live with my aunt Rachel when I was fourteen. I spent most of my time fishing.

Like I said, nothing eventful happened.

Until you went to get your aunt's money back, Delia said, not wishing to go into too much detail with her son right there.

But you got it.

Yes. I won it from Big Roy in a round of games. And I took it to her. Then three days later, I got some bait to go fishing when Big Roy's men came after me. They wanted the money back, but I couldn't let them have it.

It was Rachel's. Well, they pulled out he glanced at Johnny——K-N-I-V-E-S and chased me down an alley. Her eyes grew wide.

I never fought anybody a day in my life. I did have a KN-I-F-E because I use it to gut fish. So, I took it out to protect myself. They attacked and I panicked. It all happened so fast.

I'm not even sure exactly what happened or in what order it did. I swung you-know-what out in desperation, and it ended up in Michael's stomach. That's how he D-I-E-D.

Lance followed me out of the alley and accused me of K-I-L-L-I-N-G Michael. Which I did, but I didn't mean to.

I understand. Go on.

I panicked when I saw a lawman coming after me. I know it was dumb to run, but I wasn't thinking straight. I was so scared. So, I took my horse and headed north. Then Lance and Big Roy found me while I was taking a bath in the forest.

I didn't have time to go back for the horse or my clothes, so I ran until I came across Irving's campsite. Except I didn't know it was Irving's. I would have asked for the clothes and horse, but he wasn't anywhere in sight. Big Roy and Lance were getting closer.

I had to do something if I didn't want to die.

That's when you grabbed Irving's clothes and horse.

He nodded. Irving went after Big Roy and Lance, and I rode off. I let the horse go in Nashville and got on a train until I arrived here. I was thinking of staying here when I saw the poster of me.

Then I ran into the sheriff and was afraid he was going to arrest me. So, when he saw me in Irving's clothes and assumed I was Irving...I let him. He got new clothes for me, and before I knew it, he was taking me to the courthouse.

I kept thinking I could slip out of town and go further out west.

But then I came along needing a husband, she inserted.

I know it was wrong. I thought of telling you, but from everything I heard; Irving was this incredible man who could do anything.

And boy if he isn't. I can't compare to him. The man doesn't even need a gun to track down outlaws.

She chuckled. Neither do you. Not with that fishing rod of yours.

He grinned. Maybe. But it does look ridiculous for a deputy to run around with a fishing rod.

She kissed him on the cheek. But you managed to get the outlaws.

He put his arm around her waist and pulled her against him.

So, you forgive me?

There's nothing else I need to know?

Just that I married you because you were too beautiful to pass up. But I do love you, Delia. I want you, me, and Jeremy to be a family.

He sighed and scanned the cell. If I can get out of here.

She put her arms around him and Johnny.

There's another one on the way, Owen. That's why I was sick earlier. It wasn't because of what's happening with you. I just didn't put the pieces together until after I left with my family.

Oh, Delia. Really? That's great! He looked at Jeremy.

Now you can finally have someone to teach things like fishing.

He glanced at her and winked. Isaac's too young to understand what he teaches him.

She giggled, more from the fact that Owen was happy with the news than with Johnny wanting a brother or sister to teach.

Irving said that if I help him catch Big Roy, he'll speak on my behalf to the judge. Then maybe I can get out or serve a lesser time.

Thankfully, he's not going to charge me with stealing his horse. Did you know they hang men for that?

She frowned. Just what does Irving want you to do?

He shrugged. I don't know yet. He let go of her and set Johnny down. Sorry, buddy, but my arm is getting sore.

Can I stay here? Johnny asked, excited.

Delia couldn't believe her ears. What?

It's a real cell!

Your goal is to never be in here.

But Pa is.

She rolled her eyes, exasperated.

Owen patted him on the shoulder. Your ma is right. It's not good to be here.

I lied to a lot of people and stole some clothes and a horse. That was wrong, and now I'm paying for it.

He smiled at her. I sure am glad you came back.

We'll get through this throat.

Startled, she stepped away from Owen, wondering if one of her brothers tracked her down. But it was the sheriff.

I hope you don't mind, but I have some questions to ask Owen, the sheriff said.

No, I don't mind. She took Johnny's hand. We'll be by tomorrow with some comforts from home.

Owen nodded.

Sheriff Meyer opened the door for her and Johnny to leave.

I don't think it's as bad as it seems, he told her. Big Roy is notorious in the southern states. If we can get him, getting Owen off should be easy.

Relieved, she said, I appreciate that, Sheriff.

Then she took Johnny and left and kept going until she was out of town and heading home.

There was no way she cared to deal with her family until they calmed down enough to listen to reason, and hopefully, by the time they thought to go to her home, they'd be reasonable enough to talk to.

Chapter 18

Sandy

Delia heard Sandy knock on the front door but hesitated to answer it. No one had been out to see her since the day they found out about Owen, probably because Mary managed to talk them into giving Delia time to herself, so she didn't know why Sandy came out.

She pushed the curtain aside in the parlor. Sandy was alone. She exhaled. At least, the cavalry wasn't coming out again.

She quickly thought of a way to distract her sister from the matter at hand and opened the door while Sandy was in mid-knock.

Oh good! I wanted to talk to you. Delia pulled her into the house and peered out the door.

Good. Sandy really was alone, just as she thought. She shut the door and turned to Johnny.

Take your blocks and play upstairs. I must talk to your aunt.

Johnny obeyed and went up the steps.

As soon as he was in his room, Delia led Sandy into the kitchen and sat her down. Would you like a snack?

No thanks, Sandy said. I came to talk to you.

Yes, and I'm glad you did, Delia lied. She picked up a plate of cut up cheese and added a slice of bread to it. As long as she kept something in her stomach that she could manage to eat, she warded off the morning sickness.

How about a drink? No. I'm fine.

Delia nodded and grabbed a cup to fill with a little water.

Not too much. Just enough to help the food go down.

Delia asked Sandy how things with Rick are.

Sandy looked startled. What?

Rick? Your husband. How are things with him? She picked up the plate and cup and sat across from her sister.

You already know the answer to that.

Oh, I know that his boss hired another judge part-time and got the clerk to work full-time. But is everything still going well between you two?

Uh...yes. They are. In some ways, we're like newlyweds.

Delia caught the blush on her sister's cheeks. She grinned. So, I take it undressing in front of him worked too?

She bit into a piece of cheese.

She shrugged and stared at her hands. It didn't hurt.

Good. Now you don't have to worry about whether you're desirable anymore.

No, I don't. It's been wonderful.

Delia caught the far-off gleam in her eyes. It sure is nice to see you happy again.

Oh, I am. Why, do you believe he bought me flowers yesterday? I swear, Delia, I feel like a schoolgirl being courted all over again.

I'm glad it was nothing serious.

Me too. Now I... She stopped and frowned at her.

Wait a minute. I know what you're doing, and it won't work.

Delia swallowed another piece of cheese.

What?

You're trying to avoid talking about Owen Russell.

I am doing no such thing. She waved her hand as if to dismiss her sister's complaint and picked up the slice of bread.

I'm just curious as to the happiness of my favorite sister.

I'm your only sister.

She shrugged. You're still my favorite.

Sandy crossed her arms.

Delia took a small bite of the bread and waited to swallow it before she took a sip of water. There. Her stomach was finally settling down.

I just complimented you. This is the part where you thank me and say I'm your favorite sister too.

What's going on with Owen? You aren't really staying with him, are you?

Delia knew when she couldn't avoid her sister's badgering any longer, so she gave up trying. Giving a loud sigh, she said.

He didn't kill Michael.

Maybe not, but he did pretend to be Irving Spencer.

Who wasn't able to get here in time for me to marry him.

David kept talking about October 1st as if he planned to take Johnny on that day. At least with Owen nearby, David backed off.

Owen married you because he wanted to get into bed with you.

That's more than David did.

She groaned. Sure, Owen was wrong to lie, but honestly if I was afraid of being hanged, I'd probably do the same thing. He's only human. And for your information, he didn't sleep with me right away. He waited until I was ready.

I had to force the issue. So, if he was a horrible person, don't you think he'd have married me as Irving, had his way with me, and then headed on out? But he didn't do that. He stuck around. He must have known Irving could come into town at any time, and even then, he stayed because he wanted to be with me and Johnny.

Sandy's expression softened. Maybe.

Well, he's not going anywhere now, is he?

Because he's in jail.

No. Delia pushed her plate aside and looked pointedly at her sister. He's staying because he's owning up to his wrongs, and he'll be coming home to me and Jeremy. You'll see when it happens.

I hope you're right. She groaned and put her hand to her forehead. When her siblings harassed her like this, she could feel a headache coming on. No wonder she was desperate to get into the boarding house when she lived with her parents.

I don't mean to be hard on you, Delia. I just worry about you.

I'm fine. I'll be fine.

She rubbed her forehead. If what you fear comes to pass, then I've proven I can take care of myself and my children, haven't I?

Sandy nodded. I'm sorry, Delia. You're right.

She put her hand down and looked at her sister very surprised.

Is that unbelievable?

Well...yes.

She smiled. You're the one who told me how to get my husband's interest back. I suppose in some ways, you're older than me. It's time I started paying closer attention to what you say.

Delia relaxed. Stick around then. You might learn other things as well. Sandy laughed and picked up a piece of cheese. Maybe.

But I'll always be your older sister.

If you remember to also be a friend, I can deal with it.

Deal.

Feeling much better, Delia got more cheese.

Now shoot.

Irving said that Owen held the Colt .45 in his hands and focused on the target. He could do this. He pressed the trigger and almost fell back.

Irving chuckled and patted him on the shoulder. You need to toughen up.

Owen winced and rubbed his shoulder. The man didn't know his own strength. I did better. I hit the tree this time.

You sure did. Irving pointed to the large metal circle he'd hammered into the tree. You just need to get the bullet twelve inches closer to it, and you'll hit the edge of your target.

He sighed. There was no doubt about it. When it came to shooting a gun, he was pathetic.

You'll learn. Just need practice.

When did you learn to shoot?

Oh, I was hitting targets when I was six. Woke up one morning and mastered it by the time the day was done.

Owen's jaw dropped. And he'd been doing this for two days with little progress? Yep. He was pathetic.

Some of us are born with the shooter's eye. Others need time.

He knew that Irving meant to make him feel better but he didn't. He felt like a failure.

Now, I let word out all over about you being in Omaha.

That Big Roy should be coming to find you.

Of course, how soon he comes depends on how far he is from here. Irving smiled and rubbed his hands together. Isn't that great?

Yeah...great, Owen said, his voice void of enthusiasm.

He wiped his forehead. Despite the chill in the air, he broke into a sweat.

Big Roy...on his way to Omaha? Owen was beginning to get an inkling of what Delia was going through with her pregnancy. He felt sick to his stomach. If it'd been anyone but Aunt Rachel, he wouldn't have taken on a man with the reputation of Big Roy. I should have known he'd come after me for the money.

Why did I assume he'd be a gentleman and let things go? Irving placed his hands on his hips and took a deep breath, accentuating his broad chest. I got feelers out through town.

As soon as anyone sees Big Roy, we'll set the trap. He smiled. I can't wait!

Owen rubbed his stomach. Yes, he knew what Delia was going through.

Anyway, Irving began as he motioned to the horses, we'll stay our time. Patience will be to our advantage.

Patience wasn't a problem for Owen. He could wait for the rest of his life if need be. He placed the gun back in the holster around his waist and went to his horse.

By the way, Meyer and I decided you can go home tonight. His ears perked up.

I can?

Irving nodded. But don't run off. If you do, I'll have to put you back in the cell.

I won't.

Even though he was a sitting duck, he felt much better knowing he could be with Delia and Johnny that night. He missed them.

They'd come to visit him every day, but it wasn't the same as being at home. He eagerly hopped on the horse.

Be here tomorrow at sunrise. After we do more practice, I'll teach you how to fight.

His eyes grew wide. Fight? Isn't that what a gun is for?

Irving looked amused.

If you lose your gun, you need these. He clenched both hands into fists and held them up.

Owen gulped. The man's hands were almost as big as Owen's face.

You might be weak, but you're small. Probably quick on your feet. If you get stuck, run.

Do you ever run?

He laughed. No. But I don't have to. Of course not. The invincible Irving Spencer didn't need to resort to scurrying off like a scared rabbit.

Owen hated the fact that Irving was so competent at his job. He should have expected Irving to be that way but seeing it for himself was almost as nauseating as knowing Big Roy was out there waiting in the shadows and getting ready to ambush.

Even so, Owen had to admit that he liked Irving. The man might be the size of a monster, but he also had enough compassion to go easy on him.

Once they reached the town limits, Irving gave him a final warning about running off and then headed for the jailhouse.

Owen felt a slight sting in his gut. He wasn't a deputy anymore. Sighing, he glanced down at the spot where he had put the badge.

For some reason, he felt naked without it.

Mister?

He turned his attention to the boy who had helped him at Guy's place. Hi, Amos.

Is it true that you're not Irving Spencer? he asked, peering up at him.

Owen sighed. This wasn't fun. He knew the boy looked up to him to Irving Spencer as a hero, and he hated to dash the boy's hopes.

Taking a deep breath, he admitted, Yes, it's true. I'm really Owen Russell.

To his surprise, the boy broke into a wide grin. Then it's also true you're on the run from a big-time outlaw?

He wasn't sure how to respond but finally figured the truth would be best. After all, look at how much trouble lying had caused.

Yes, Big Roy is looking for me.

Because you killed one of his men?

Well, that man and his brother came after me with knives.

Were the men big?

Owen thought about it for a moment. Bigger than me but not as big as Irving.

You took on two of them at once?

He shrugged. —Well...yes. I did. They followed me down the alley and had me cornered.

And all you had was a knife?

He nodded. I didn't have a gun. It was good I had to go fishing that day or else I wouldn't have had it. I used that knife to gut fish.

Wow.

He wrinkled his eyebrows. Wow?

The boy waved his two friends over. Two big men chased him down an alley and tried to kill him, but he got away!

The other boys looked impressed as they approached him.

Do you have the knife on you? one asked.

No, Owen replied, still surprised. It had blood all over it so I left it behind.

Blood? Was there a lot of it?

Owen thought for a moment. His shirt soaked up most of it, but I guess there was a good-sized stain on his shirt before he fell to the ground.

Then what happened? Amos asked.

I ran out of the alley, Owen replied.

Did the other bad guy come after you?

Yes, and he wasn't happy. There was no way he could forget the look of outrage on Lance's face. He even got a lawman to go after me.

You outran the sheriff?

I panicked.

But you were fast, huh? You had to be fast! Another boy said, nudging his friend in the arm with an excited expression on his face.

Owen felt a chuckle rise in his throat. Well, being short helps, you run fast.

And you fooled Sheriff Meyer!

Now wait. Lying is wrong. I didn't do the right thing.

He had to make that clear to them in case they thought it was a good idea to do that in the future.

Oh, we know. We heard you got put into prison.

Right. And I belonged there for what I did.

But you're out now.

Owen nodded. Because the sheriff and deputy decided to give me another chance. I must help them catch Big Roy.

Big Roy is coming here? Amos said, nearly jumping up and down.

It's a sure thing. He's coming after me.

Wow! Big Roy is coming here! Another boy said.

Amos smiled with obvious glee. And all because of you!

You must be important, the boy agreed.

Owen hadn't thought of it that way, nor did he think he was deserved their praise.

But he could see that this gave them something fun to talk about. He might as well make the most of it.

Now, you three remember to be honest. It's much better to be Irving Spencer than Owen Russell. Irving is always honest, and he gets the outlaws each time.

With your help, Amos added.

He raised an eyebrow at the three excited boys. Alright.

So, they would insist on hailing him as a hero of sorts. What was the harm in that if they understood they shouldn't go around lying? Just to make sure, he asked, you do know lying is wrong, don't you?

Oh yes, sir, Amos replied. We don't want to get in trouble like you did.

Owen furrowed his eyebrows. Then why are you looking at me as if I'm a hero?

Because you came clean, one of the boys said. You're on the good side now.

Owen couldn't argue with their logic. Alright.

We'll be on the lookout for Big Roy and let you know if we see him, Amos promised.

He smiled. Be sure to do that. We will.

After they said good-bye and ran off, Owen watched them, thinking maybe things were going to be alright after all. At least regarding his reputation.

CHAPTER 19

Out of Jail

Johnny ran to the front door and jumped into Owen's arms.

Surprised, Delia turned from the sandwiches she'd been making and went over to him.

They let you out of jail?

As long as I promised not to run away. He gave Johnny a big hug. I missed you, squirt.

Was it scary in there? Johnny asked.

No, but it was lonely. It's good to be home with my family. He leaned forward and gave Delia a kiss.

I can't believe how much I missed you two. We missed you too, she said, hugging him as much as she could with Johnny between them.

I was just making supper.

Are you hungry?

I didn't get much to eat, so yes. He set Johnny down and took off his coat and hat.

It's nothing fancy. Just sandwiches, she warned.

He put up his holster on the hook next to his coat and hat.

After eating nothing but beans and jerky, sandwiches will be a treat. He turned to them and gave them another hug. It feels so good to be back home.

She laughed and hugged him back. It's nice to have you home.

I finished the doghouse, Johnny said.

With a little help, Delia whispered, holding onto Owen's waist.

He put his arm around her waist and asked Johnny, does the dog like it?

Sure does. He slept in there last night, Johnny answered. Want to see it?

You bet I do. He turned to her and kissed her again.

I'll be right back.

Sighing, she released him. She didn't want to let him go but figured it was for a good cause. Alright. But you better hurry back.

Honey, there's nowhere else I'd rather be. He let go of her and put his coat back on.

You'll need a coat too. He handed Johnny his coat.

I'll have sandwiches done by the time you return, she promised.

Sounds good. He gave her a wink before he followed Johnny out the front door.

Delia groaned as Owen deepened the kiss. She didn't think Johnny would never get to sleep. But he finally did, and now she had Owen all to herself.

Alone in their bedroom...and being able to do what she'd been aching to do ever since he came home.

How she missed this. Having his hands caress parts of her that made her body tingle in places no one else was allowed to touch. Having his lips travel down her neck. Having his tongue teased, he lightly traced her ear. She shivered in delight and ran her hand down his chest until it settled on his erection. Even through his pants, he felt wonderful.

He moaned and pulled slightly away from her. We need to get out of these clothes.

Bringing his hands up to her shirt, he began to unbutton it.

She undid his belt and pants. Sliding her hand under the soft fabric of his underwear, she stroked him. —Hmm... I missed you.

Not as much as I missed you, I bet. He finished unbuttoning her shirt and cupped her breasts through the thin chemise.

You feel good, Delia.

She kissed him. Her tongue ran the length of his lower lip until he opened his mouth and let her in. It seemed like weeks instead of days since he'd last made love to her. Her body ached for him.

All her years of sexual abstention were quickly catching up to her.

As much as she hated to break the physical contact with him, she withdrew her hand from his pants so she could shrug off her shirt.

She let out a contented sigh as he kissed her neck.

Owen, she murmured. Owen Russell. Not Irving Owen Spencer. But she got to meet Irving, albeit briefly, and knew Owen Russell was better suited for her. Delia Russell.

That was the first time she thought of her new last name, and she liked it.

Mrs. Owen Russell. She wanted to make love to him as Delia Russell instead of Delia Spencer.

She broke contact with him to fully undress. Even though the room was chilly, her flesh was warm under the appreciative stare of her husband. Giving him a modest smile, she asked. Like what you see? knowing full well that he did.

What's not to like? You're perfect.

Oh, Owen. You know all the right words to say. She settled on the bed and raised an eyebrow.

Are you going to stand there watching me all night or are you going to join me?

She patted the spot next to her.

He blinked, as if he hadn't considered the possibility, and shrugged out of his clothes before he got into bed next to her.

I must admit this gets more and more exciting each time we do it.

She giggled and drew him closer to her. Without giving him a chance to say anything else, she brought her lips to his and wrapped her legs around his waist. I need you, she whispered and wiggled against him.

He entered her and groaned. I missed you, Delia.

He reached for her hands and clasped them over her head.

She moved her hips, thinking of how good it felt when he was inside her. He moved in rhythm with her. The ache grew stronger, and she figured she should take her time to savor each thrust but her body wouldn't have it.

She rolled on top of him and sighed in pleasure.

Lovemaking had been incredible in the past, and this time was no exception.

She reached the peak sooner than she anticipated. Her body tensed as she cried out, and shortly, he joined her.

They remained still for a few moments, and she delighted in each lingering wave that went through her until she was satisfied. She looked down at him and saw that he was smiling at her. Smiling in return, she leaned forward and kissed him, this time gentle and slow.

You sure are one passionate woman, he murmured as he squeezed her hips.

It helps to have something to be passionate about. She got off him, grabbed a blanket, and snuggled against him.

He wrapped her in his arms and kissed the top of her head. I love you, Delia. I want you to know that no matter what happens when Big Roy gets to town, I love you, Johnny, and the baby.

She lifted her head. After the wonderful moment they'd just shared, he thought to bring up something this dismal? Don't think that way. You'll help Irving get him. Then you'll come home and spend the rest of your life making love to me.

When she saw the worried look in his eyes, she continued. Think positive, Owen. You can do it. You just must start believing in yourself. When you won your aunt's money back, what were you thinking?

That I didn't have any choice but to win. I couldn't let Aunt Rachel down.

Then think of how much Johnny and I need you. You have no choice but to win this time too.

You're right. He gave her a slight squeeze. I will.

She settled her head on his chest and closed her eyes.

I will, he whispered.

Owen was on his way to meet up with Irving for another round of shooting when he ran into Jenny's brothers. His steps slowed as he approached the jailhouse.

He thought of getting right back on his horse and heading back to the safety of his home where Delia had managed to keep her kin at bay.

This was ridiculous. He couldn't hide behind a woman's skirts for the rest of his life even if they were his wife's...and even if his life might be cut short by Big Roy.

He took a deep breath. Nope. It was time to be a man and confront four brothers who still looked angry. Are you aware that people are saying you're daring Big Roy to find you? Richard asked, his arms crossed.

Owen's jaw dropped. Wh-what? I don't think it's wise for you to brag on how you outwitted him.

I'm not bragging! Like he'd ever evoke the wrath of Big Roy!

Irving Spencer let me out of jail in hopes that he'd come to kill me. It's not something I'm looking forward to.

Tom rubbed his chin. He does look scared.

Joel nodded thoughtfully. Kind of like a mouse being chased by a cat.

Owen wiped his forehead. Even when a layer of fresh snow covered the ground, he could break into a sweat.

Who's saying that I'm boasting like that?

Just about everyone, Richard said.

Stevie furrowed his eyebrows in concern. Do you need to sit down? You look pale.

Owen drew a shaky breath and sat on the bench in front of the jailhouse. Look, I love Delia. I'm not going to leave her. I know I married her for the wrong reason, but I'm not sorry I married her.

He shook his head. I'm not sticking around because I'm looking forward to seeing Big Roy again.

I think he means it, Stevie said.

It does look like it, Tom replied.

Maybe we should go easy on him, Joel added.

Richard gave a slight nod, as if his decision settled the matter, and said, Alright. I believe him too.

Owen hid the urge to roll his eyes. He couldn't stand it when people talked about him as if he wasn't there.

As if Owen hadn't just heard them, Richard leaned forward and said, we believe you.

You don't hear the rumors about you? Joel asked.

Owen gritted his teeth. Well, I've been in prison up until yesterday.

That is true, Richard said. Just so you know, word is that you're bragging on how you outsmarted Big Roy.

Apparently, you have a stash of the money you won in the game hidden somewhere around here.

The blood drained from Owen's face. Big Roy thought he had the money? He tried to swallow but his throat was too dry.

This was worse than he thought! Big Roy would be coming after him for sure!

Joel grabbed him by the shoulder to steady him. Hey, you aren't going to faint, are you?

I thought only women fainted, Richard said.

Well, he is wanted by a notorious murderer from the south, Tom replied. And it's obvious he's not ready for what's coming. I heard he can't shoot a target to save his life.

Owen didn't think it was possible, but this made him feel even worse. That piece of information was going around town too? Oh God, I'm a sitting duck!

Great, Richard grumbled. This is a fine how-do-you do. He got Jenny in the family way and now he's going to get himself shot! He glared at Owen. Couldn't you have at least pretended to be Irving in all situations? Then she wouldn't have another mouth to feed.

Stevie tapped his older brother on the arm. To be fair, it should have occurred to her that something wasn't right.

I don't get it, Joel whispered. How can someone as big as Irving not he glanced around you know.

What? Tom asked.

Are you kidding me? Joel turned to Tom. You still haven't figured it out?

It doesn't matter, Richard inserted. What matters is what we're going to do with Owen's dead body and how we're going to help Delia out. You know how proud she is. She rarely accepts help from anyone.

Just dump him out in the fields and let the animals get him, Joel said.

No, Stevie replied. We need to bury him. It's not right to let a corpse rot like that.

I guess we can dig a hole in the ground. Joel snapped his fingers. We'll do it on Neil's property. No one cares about going out there anyway.

Owen bolted to his feet. I'm not dead yet. He shook his head. I mean, I don't plan on dying.

They looked at him, as if suddenly remembering he was right in front of them.

A bunch of fine brothers-in-law you all turned out to be!

Owen huffed. I got away from Big Roy once and I'll do it again. Richard frowned. By running off to another town?

If I must. Before they could protest, he pointed a finger at them. But I'll take Delia and Johnny with me.

Irving opened the door to the jailhouse and stepped outside.

They immediately stopped and turned to him.

Time for shooting practice, Irving told Owen.

Like it'll do any good, Joel muttered.

Owen decided he'd had enough. For your information, I can handle myself just fine. I'll survive this. And when I do, I'll be ready to accept all your apologies.

Grunting, he strode over to Irving and glared at them. The nerve of the lot of them trying to off him before his time! Sure, Big Roy might get him, but he didn't need Delia's brothers arranging his burial, as dishonoring as it was.

Irving patted Owen's shoulder. I assure you that I'll be here when Big Roy comes. I won't let him die.

Owen winced and rubbed his shoulder. The four brothers glanced uneasily at Irving before they agreed with him and quickly headed off.

Owen wished he could get rid of them that easily. But no. He had to be lanky and short which made them feel justified in giving him a hard time. At least Jenny liked him the way he was.

Ready to go to the shooting range?

Owen nodded. Pulling his coat tighter around him, he followed Irving to their horses.

CHAPTER 20

Big Roy

It was a week later when Big Roy finally arrived in Omaha. And Owen had just finished breakfast when the fateful knock came at the door.

He put his napkin down and went to answer it. Amos? he asked, surprised to see the boy with his two friends standing on his porch, holding fishing rods. Isn't it a little cold to be fishing?

It was December after all. Big Roy's in Omaha, Amos said, looking unusually excited by the prospect.

Owen's eyes grew wide. How do you know this?

We saw him. Oh, he's big and angry alright. He was asking where you were.

You didn't tell him, did you? Owen demanded as he watched the boy practically dance with glee. Was everyone but Delia and Johnny eager to send him to an early grave?

Course not! We'd never do that, Amos assured him.

In fact, no one's telling him anything. But Irving wants you down at the jailhouse. Amos motioned to his fishing rod. You don't need to worry about a thing. We're ready to help you!

Amos and his friends thrust the fishing rods forward, almost hitting him in the face with them.

Alright, Owen uncertainly said. He gently pushed the fishing rods back. You three need to be careful. Big Roy isn't one to mess with. He's a dangerous man.

We know! another boy said with a big grin. I hear he killed two guards when he got out of prison. He didn't even need a weapon. He just used his bare hands.

Wonderful. Terrific. Just what Owen wanted to hear! He was sure the boy was exaggerating...but still... He shivered.

Delia walked over to him as she wiped her hands on a towel. What is it? She glanced at the boys and smiled. Hello.

Big Roy is in town Owen whispered to her. Turning to the boys, he said, You better go on home to your mothers.

They'll want you to be safe.

Oh, alright. Amos winked at him before he and his friends darted across the grass to their horses.

Delia gave him a curious look. What was that about?

He rolled his eyes. They think they're going to help me.

I told them to go home.

She pulled him close to her. Remember what I said.

He nodded. I'm doing this for you and Johnny, he said softly. Holding her face in his hands, he kissed her, praying this wouldn't be the last time he'd get to do so. I love you.

I love you too. And you'll make it. You have a family to come back to.

Walking over to Johnny who had been taking his time with eating the eggs on his plate, Owen picked him up and gave him a tight hug. I love you, squirt.

I love you too, Pa.

Fighting back his tears, Owen set his son down and headed to the hooks by the door so he could grab his gun and holster to slip around his waist. It wasn't easy to fasten it with his shaky hands but he managed.

Then, he slipped on his coat and put his hat on his head. Turning to a worried looking Delia, he said, this is it.

She ran over to him and gave him another hug.

Remember to be positive.

He nodded and tightened his hold on her, noting the sweet scent of honey soap in her hair and the softness of her skin.

Funny how such details became vivid in that instant, but maybe that's what happened when a man wondered if he'd ever see his wife again. Before she could catch him crying, he wiped his eyes and then pulled away from her. Clasping her hands, he took a deep breath. I'll be back.

Even though he suspected she wondered about it as much as he did, she agreed.

After another kiss, he reluctantly left to get his horse. As he rode off the property, he glanced back one more time to see Delia and Johnny watching him from the porch. I must do this for them. I can do it. Looking forward, he exhaled. I have to do this.

By the time Owen reached town, he'd said his final prayers to make amends for anything bad he'd done in his life, figuring it couldn't hurt to have the slate clean if he was about to meet his maker. Too late he thought of a will, but then, he didn't really have anything to his name, so he had nothing to leave Delia and Johnny.

So, as far as he was concerned, he had everything settled and could leave this life in peace. He'd done all he could do.

Now, it was up to fate to handle the details, no matter how grim those details might be. He sighed. He didn't fancy himself a pessimist, but he supposed a man facing the possibility of death was permitted a glass half empty' moment.

As he turned the corner of the block that would take him to the jailhouse, Sheriff Meyer waved him over to the side of the street. Owen obeyed and got off his horse.

The sheriff took the reins for him. Big Roy must have a connection in town. We don't know where he's hiding, but rumor is that he was with one of the saloon girls last night.

By the time I got there, he was gone. We thought if you walked around a bit, he might come out of hiding. Might as well start with a walk past the saloon.

Even though he didn't want to, Owen gave the obligatory glance over his shoulder at where the saloon was located.

Irving's in that area. He's going to be watching you.

Once Big Roy pops up, the action begins.

Sounds fun, Owen blandly replied.

You're in good hands. Irving's the best there is.

So, he'd heard. Again, and again.

The sheriff cleared his throat. It hasn't been the same without you.

Owen wasn't sure he heard right. Sheriff?

The man shrugged. Just had fun joking around, that's all. He patted him on the shoulder. Maybe if you get through this, we can have two deputies.

But I lied.

You served your sentence. And you learned your lesson, right?

Sure, I did.

Good. Then there's a slot open for you. Just as Owen was ready to thank him, he continued, that is, if you survive.

Owen's smile faltered. Right. There was that tiny staying alive thing. Without delaying the inevitable, he turned in the direction he needed to go.

Son, the sheriff called out.

Owen stopped.

Don't forget that gun of yours.

Oh, right. Owen put his hand on his holster. The gun wasn't as comfortable as a fishing rod, but he supposed he couldn't keep on carrying that around forever. The gun still felt unnatural in his hand, but at least he figured out how to use it.

Maybe not as good as Irving did, but it was better than what he used to do. Here goes nothing, he murmured under his breath before he crossed the street.

He could barely hear people chatting around him as he passed them by on the boardwalk lining the businesses.

The pounding in his ears was much too distracting. But what did it matter what they were saying? Soon enough, they might be looking at his dead body and wondering why he thought he had any chance against a big-time outlaw like Big Roy.

He took a deep breath to clear his head and wiped the sweat from his brow. This was it. Soon, it would all be over. No more running. No more hiding.

As he approached the saloon, his grip tightened on the butt of his gun and his steps slowed. He peered into the window and saw a couple of men lounging around at the bar. None were Big Roy, or anyone associated with him. His shoulders relaxed, but only slightly.

Big Roy was in Omaha...somewhere. He scanned the people who mingled about. He didn't recognize anyone in there. He didn't even see where Irving was hiding.

If Irving was even watching him... He wiped his forehead again. Of course, Irving was watching. He took his job seriously, and he wanted to bring Big Roy to justice.

Owen had to admit, though, that Irving did an excellent job of hiding.

Unsure of what to do, he continued moving forward. A couple of women giggled as he past them.

Wondering if his fear showed, he looked to see if they were laughing at him. But they weren't. They were pointing to something across the street.

Curious, his gaze traveled to where they motioned to and his jaw dropped.

Amos and his friends were lingering by the mercantile eating some candy and holding onto their fishing rods.

Owen's jaw clenched, and he quickly checked both ways before he stepped onto the street. Didn't he just tell them to go home and stay safe? He made it halfway across the street when the first gunshot rang out and blew the hat off his head.

The boys looked up at him in surprise.

Get out of here! he yelled at them as he darted past a startled horse with an equally startled rider.

Another gunshot broke through the still air, but this one didn't come near him. Or maybe it did, and he was too scared to notice. Either way, he needed to get out of there! And he wasn't the only one who thought that way. Everyone else scattered for whatever shelter they could find.

Some ran into the stores and some down alleyways. Some rode their horses and buggies as fast as they could until the street was clear of all traffic.

Owen found himself bolting into the mercantile. He tried to take out his gun, but the stupid thing was secured in the holster and the palms of his hands were too slippery to get a hold of it.

He scanned the mercantile at the frightened women and children, but he didn't see Amos or his two friends. Didn't they run in here?

You're mine!

Owen recognized that gruff voice anywhere. And there was no way he was going to play possum now. He leapt over the counter, nearly knocking over the startled owner who ran to retrieve his gun.

This is my store. You have no business being here! The owner barked. Then he fired his rifle at the doorway.

Owen didn't bother seeing if the man hit Big Roy or not.

He just ran. He ran down the narrow space that led to the backdoor and found himself in another alley.

The scene was eerily familiar. Except this time Michael and Lance weren't chasing him.

Nope. Big Roy was doing the honors this time.

Owen raced past the dumpsters. He heard a door open and almost got hit with a bullet. He swerved to the right and found himself on a less traveled part of the business district.

He bent to hide behind stagecoaches and buggies as he scampered as fast as he dared without giving Big Roy ample opportunity to get a clear shot.

Where was Irving anyway? Some stellar deputies he was turning out to be! Owen had already been shot at three times and Big Roy was still chasing him.

He found a vacant stagecoach that was still on the side of the road, so he slipped into it and curled up on the floor. He pressed his hand to his aching side and gasped.

He could barely catch his breath. He shook his head to make the rushing sound in his ears die down. There were voices approaching and he needed to hear who they were from.

We need to get out of here, an unfamiliar man said.

We can pick them up later.

The other man agreed, and the stagecoach swayed, shoving Owen from side to side since the man driving it was in a hurry.

Who could blame him? Owen was anxious to get out of there as well. He hesitated to see if Big Roy was out there but finally decided he might have an advantage if he knew.

Finding his balance, he leaned against the seat to peek out the window. His eyes grew wide. Irving was pursuing them on a horse.

What in the world was Irving doing chasing him? Irving made eye contact with Owen and gave some gestures that Owen didn't understand. Just as Owen shook his head, Big Roy's head popped into view from above the stagecoach.

Big Roy gave Owen a sinister smile.

Owen screamed and scrambled back. The driver suddenly stopped the stagecoach and the door behind Owen's back flew open.

Still screaming and probably sounding just like a woman. Owen went barreling down the side of the hill. He stopped screaming so he could grunt and groan each time his body hit a rock that was poking out of the ground.

Several gunshots sounded, and all Owen could do was pray none of them would hit him as he tossed and turned, his world spinning out of control around him.

When Owen did manage to come to a stop, he saw another horse rider coming in his direction and recognized him as one of Big Roy's men. That man also had two other riders with him.

Gasping, Owen struggled to his feet and ran further into the trees that surrounded the perimeter of the park.

Up ahead, he saw a small bridge and scrambled under it. It was a tight fit, but he managed it. Then he waited.

The three men assembled near the bridge and stopped.

Where did he go?

Owen turned his head to better listen to them. If he heard right, that was David Jenkins. But what would David want with him?

Weasels are sneaky, another replied.

That was Jim, one of the card players at the saloon in Louisiana and one of Big Roy's friends. Owen fought the urge to sneeze. He squeezed his eyes shut tight and pinched his nose.

Look, Jim said. You two need to move fast unless you want to push up daisies like Owen will be in a few minutes.

Right. We'll get that boy. Right, David?

Owen's eyelids flew open. Were they talking about Johnny?

You don't get him this time and you'll be working the mines, Jim said. This has gone on long enough. You owe Big Roy.

I know, David said. I'll get him.

And I'll go to make sure you do it right this time.

Go on, Robert. I got Owen, Jim replied.

Robert! That was the man wanted for kidnapping children. His eyes grew wide. Big Roy had a mining operation that was driven by childhood labor? He gasped. Johnny! Delia!

Owen finally grabbed his gun and pulled it out. He had to get to them before David and Robert did.

He waited until the men rode off before he crept out of his hiding spot. Holding the gun firmly in his hand, he found the nearest horse a good half mile away lounging by its rider.

Well, drastic times called for drastic measures. He headed for the horse and made it close to the pathway when a bullet skinned the sleeve of his coat.

Thrown off guard, he stumbled and fell beneath one of the trees in the shaded area. He scrambled in the dirt until he got behind one of the trees that was big enough to protect him from several more shots.

Gripping the gun, he peered around the edge of the trunk and saw Jim riding toward him. He ducked before another bullet went flying. I must get to Delia and Johnny!

He poked his head out again and aimed the gun and fired it. Jim's horse bucked a bit, but Jim quickly regained control.

Licking his lips, Owen steadied his hand and made another attempt to shoot Jim or the horse, but Jim shot the gun right out of Owen's hand.

Owen yelped and pulled his hand to his chest and hid behind the tree. He quickly inspected his hand.

One, two, three, four, five. All fingers were there. He wiggled them. He breathed a sigh of relief.

That was lucky. A sudden neigh and angry yell took Owen's focus off his hand. He peered around the tree. He blinked and rubbed his eyes. He looked again.

So, he wasn't seeing things. Jim was hanging beneath a tree by three fishing hooks that were dug firmly into the back of his shirt. Owen's gaze traveled up the tree, and he saw the proud smiles of three very happy looking boys.

Amos? he said in a mixture of awe and disbelief.

We got them for you, deputy!

Amos hollered out. Yep, another boy stated, we fished him right out for you, just like you would!

After a moment of stunned silence, Owen laughed. Now that's the finest bit of fishing I ever saw. Great job, boys!

He found Jim's gun lying on a small patch of snow and picked it up.

Glancing up, he saw that Irving was heading toward them, but he was still a good distance away.

Obviously, he managed to capture Big Roy. Turning to the boys, Owen said, Tell Irving Spencer that I had to help Delia and Johnny.

Without waiting for the boys to respond, he ran up to Jim's horse which had slowed down to a walk not too far from them and got on it to head home.

CHAPTER 21

Fighting David

Delia flung a dish at David's head. Drats! She missed! Get off my property!

She picked up another plate from the stack she held to her chest and threw it at him.

Again, he expertly dodged it as he made his way to the porch. She grunted and threw the whole stack at him.

This time two plates hit him in the face. He yelled and touched his cheek which had a bloody cut on it. Glaring at her, he took a step toward her. Not this time, Delia! I'm getting my son.

She grabbed her broom and swung at him. Unlike last time, he jumped back.

She stepped forward but someone came up behind her and held her arms in place.

She screamed and kicked at her captor, but his hold only grew tighter.

Get the boy and let's get out of here, the man growled at David.

Run! she yelled at Jeremy who was supposed to be in his room. She prayed he would make it to the attic before David found him.

David climbed the rest of the porch steps, and as he passed her, she stuck her foot out so he tripped and fell on his face, hitting the doorway with the side of his head.

Then she bent forward and bit the other man on the arm. He roared and let her go. She gripped the broom and swiped it under his feet, so he fell.

Knowing her time to act was short, she hopped over Clyde and kicked him so he wasn't in the doorway and slammed the door on his face.

She locked the door and ran up the staircase.

Ma? a terrified voice asked.

She turned to Johnny who huddled in the corner of his room. Get into the attic, she whispered.

I can't. It's too high.

One of the men smashed the window in the parlor. She jumped and saw her son's terrified eyes. What were they doing here? Why did David want Jeremy so badly?

Trembling, she darted into the room and flung the window open. Looking out of it, she breathed a sigh of relief.

Owen had forgotten to take down the ladder when he fixed the shutter by the window.

Go down the ladder and hide in the barn loft. Okay?

He nodded. She gave him a quick hug, said she loved him, and helped him get his footing steady on the ladder before she turned her attention back to the men invading her home.

She hurried to her room and opened the armoire. Up on the top shelf was a rifle.

Snatching it, she returned to the top of the staircase and saw the men rummaging through the house.

They threw over the couch and chair in the parlor as they searched for her boy.

She hadn't used a gun since she went after the foxes trying to get into the hen house on her parent's farm, but there was no time like the present to home in on old skills.

She fired a shot which went right through the front door. The men weren't even close to it, but they stopped and stared at her, so she got their attention.

Get out of my home before I kill you! She fired the gun again, and this time, the bullet went into the kitchen floor.

She gritted her teeth. Why couldn't she even get the bullet into the parlor? She knew she was rusty, but this was ridiculous.

David's face was pale, and he held his hands up, but the other man smirked at her and drew out his gun.

You don't know how to use that thing.

Sure, I do, she lied. Those were warning shots! Uh huh.

By the tone in his voice, she knew he didn't believe her. He rubbed his pistol along his jaw and sauntered to the threshold of the kitchen. Where's the boy?

Long gone. Now get out! She lifted the rifle to her eye and tried to gauge where to shoot him.

He flipped the pistol in his hand and shot the top of the banister which was a mere five inches from her elbow.

She yelped and almost dropped her rifle.

I didn't miss, sweetheart. That was my warning. Now, tell me where the boy is or I'll make sure he loses his mama.

Tears stung her eyes and she glared at David.

What do you want with him?

Where is he? the other man barked.

The front door flew open, and Owen charged into the kitchen. Hands up!

David obeyed.

The other man rolled his eyes. I've handled worse. The boy belongs to Big Roy. David over there he motioned to the trembling man who looked as if he was ready to pass out lost to Roy in game of poker.

He couldn't he opted to give up the boy. Now, hand him over.

No! Delia screamed. Never! She fired again and got within ten inches of shooting Owen's foot.

Over there! Owen said, shocked.

I was aiming over there, she replied through her tears.

Let me handle this, Delia, Owen said in a voice that told her he knew what he was doing. I've been trained for this.

She nodded at him but kept her rifle up and ready to shoot just in case the man got any ideas about shooting her to distract Owen.

Owen directed his gaze at the man and kept his gun pointed at him. The sheriff's on his way, and he's bringing Irving Spencer with him. You're familiar with Irving Spencer, aren't you? He's the best deputy around. You can't stand up against him.

By the time they get here, I'll be long gone. In a swift movement, he directed his gun at Owen.

Owen pulled his trigger first and shot him in the chest.

Delia gasped and almost dropped her rifle, but she quickly renewed her grip.

The man dropped his pistol and fell to the floor. A moment of tense silence hung in the air before Owen directed the gun at David.

Don't shoot, David whimpered and held his hands up higher. Please don't shoot. I don't want to die.

The sheriff and Irving stumbled into the house and studied the scene.

Did you do this? Sheriff Meyer asked Owen.

David lowered the rifle. That man was going to shoot him! And me! And he and David were going to take Johnny to Big Roy.

Owen was defending us! She knew she was rambling and yelling, but she was too shaken up to be calm or silent. He's a hero.

Owen's gaze met hers and he smiled. At that moment, she relaxed and returned his smile. He really was a hero. Who needed Irving Spencer when she had Owen Russell to defend her and Johnny?

It sure looks like you're a hero to me, the sheriff agreed.

Yep, Irving said and patted Owen on the back.

Owen lurched forward but stopped before he fell on his face.

Who knew you had it in you? Irving said.

Finally able to move, Delia descended the staircase. She placed the rifle on the table and hugged her husband. You did do a great job, Owen! I'm so proud of you.

Looking pleased, he pulled her close to his side. Once I had it in my head that I needed to be there for you and Johnny, the rest just fell into place.

He glanced out the doorway and called out, Johnny? It's safe!

You know where he hid?

I saw him come down the ladder and found a couple of thick bushes for him to hide.

Well, you did a fine job, the sheriff said with a big smile.

A very fine job.

Johnny ran into the house and into Delia's arms.

She held the boy tightly. Thank you, Owen. She meant that for more than what he did that day. For he was more than the man who saved her son. He was also a real father to him.

Together, they were a real family. Just as she used to dream of but feared would never come to pass once, she messed things up with David.

The sheriff grabbed Clyde by the arm.

Time to reap what you've sown, young man. Delia didn't even look at David as he and the sheriff left.

Instead, she pressed her face against Johnny's blond hair and gave her thanks that David would no longer be a problem.

I'll decide for Robert's body. Irving lifted the body as if it was no heavier than a bag of potatoes.

You did good, Owen. Real good. Then he left.

It was about time Delia's brothers stopped their harassment, Owen thought as they took in the bright, shiny deputy badge that Sheriff Meyer returned to him.

Owen's chest puffed up with a sense of pride as he closed the door of the jailhouse and placed his hat on his head.

Good afternoon, gentlemen, he said and buttoned his coat.

Getting ready for Christmas?

We had some errands to run, Tom replied. Even if women say they don't want anything but our love, they don't mean it.

Joel snickered. You must learn that the hard way.

Tom's face grew red. I can't wait until you get married, Joel. I don't care what you argue about. I'll take her side each time.

Unlike you all, I have no desire to tie the knot, he replied and gave them a smug smile. I'm going to stay single forever.

Since when?

Since I saw how you all ended up. No woman is going to tell me what to do.

Oh really? Stevie asked.

Then what are you doing in town looking for gifts? Joel sighed. I got to give a gift to Ma. When he saw their amused expressions, he said, But Ma doesn't count.

She's a woman, Richard dryly pointed out.

Not a womanly woman. She's just...Ma.

I wonder what she'd think if she heard that, Tom mused.

She won't mind. Joel shrugged and kicked at a rock on the boardwalk. She loves me no matter what.

The brothers rolled their eyes but turned their attention back to Owen.

So anyway, Richard began, while we were in town, we thought we'd apologize. You know, for hounding you and all.

Yeah, Tom added. Guess we were wrong about you.

Owen placed his hand on the butt of his gun that was resting in the holster. Just remember that. I'm on the right side of the law now.

Tom's gaze flickered to the Colt .45. Well, you weren't the deputy when we came after you, so that time doesn't count.

You were ready to write my obituary, Owen reminded him.

The four men stood silent, as if trying to determine just what, exactly, Owen was going to do.

Deciding that he'd messed with them long enough, Owen chuckled and twirled the gun in his hand. They ducked.

He laughed harder and placed the gun back in the holster.

You're all too easy. It's alright. I forgive you. The door behind him opened and Irving stepped out.

Leaving already? Owen asked, noting his travel bag.

Irving nodded. Texas needs a lawman who's dedicated to his job. I hear it can be rough out in that area. I hope that's true.

After Irving complained that catching Big Roy and the others weren't challenging enough, Owen wasn't surprised that he started looking for other places to go to. Hope those outlaws down there keep you on your toes.

Nice meeting you, Owen. He shook Owen's hand before he tipped his hat to our brothers who moved out of his way.

Owen waited until Irving was out of hearing distance and said, yep. Way too easy to scare you all. But all the same, I look forward to seeing you at the family gathering on Christmas day.

Right now, I must pick up my aunt from the train station.

The one you got the money for? Richard asked.

That's the only one I got.

You know, it was nice of you to do that, Stevie said.

Pretty brave too, Tom added.

I mean, I saw Big Roy. He's not the kind I'd want to go up against.

I'll agree with Tom on this one, Joel replied.

Richard smiled. Well, we think Delia s lucky to have you.

A man who'd go against the likes of Big Roy for those he loves is alright with us.

Pleased, Owen said his thanks. He then left them and hopped on over to pick up his aunt.

The train pulled into the station just as he arrived. Though it hadn't been more than three months since he last saw Rachel, it seemed like a year.

She pulled him in for one of her bear hugs. You're a sight for sore eyes.

How are you doing?

She patted him on the back twice before she let him go.

Good because of you.

So, everything's alright down in the bayou?

Yes. It was still a foolish thing you did. I heard all these rumors about you killing a man, but I knew you wouldn't hurt a fly.

I explained it all in my letter.

You sure did. Said you have a wife, a son, and a young's on the way?

Yep. He collected her travel bag and took her by the arm. Delia is making a big meal for you. She wanted to come, but she's still fighting off nausea from expecting.

Poor thing. Well, I got just the thing to help with that.

You know we use lots of spices in our cooking down south. I have a feeling she'll like ginger.

He smiled. She's a great girl. I think you'll like her, and that boy of hers is going to be a fine fisherman if I have anything to say about it.

She chuckled as they left the train station. I have no doubt both are fine.

He led her to his buggy and took her home.

A new layer of snow covered the ground, giving it a special wintery feel. He couldn't have asked for a better welcome for his aunt than this.

He set the brake and helped his aunt out of the buggy before he grabbed her bag.

She shivered. How do you handle this cold?

You get used to it. Especially when one has a nice warm body in bed to hold, but he figured some things were best left unsaid.

Are you sure you don't want to move up here? She rolled her eyes. Now I know you aren't right in the head. You bring me up here when it's cold and ask that?

He shrugged. It's just nice having you here.

She grinned and patted him on the shoulder. I have enough money to come visit when the mood strikes.

Next time I'm coming in the summer though.

Chuckling, he opened the front door. The smell of pinecone coming from the wreath Delia made soaked the room.

The Christmas tree in the corner of the parlor and lit fireplace gave the whole house a festive feel.

Owen found he enjoyed the season a lot more with Delia there to decorate the place. He recalled his little shack along the swamp and didn't miss it a single bit.

Pa! Johnny came running from the parlor and jumped into Owen's arms.

Hey there, squirt. He hugged the boy. This is Aunt Rachel.

I'm five, he told her.

That's true, Owen replied. He had a birthday last week.

We'll have to do something special while I'm here, she told the boy.

Are you keeping my nephew here out of trouble?

Oh yes, ma'am. He hasn't had any falls since Aunt Sandy and Uncle Rick were here.

She glanced at Owen. You had a fall?

It was nothing. I'll tell you about it later. He set the boy down. Where's your ma?

Right here. Delia laughed as she came down the steps.

You must be Owen's aunt.

Rachel nodded. That's what my brother told me when Owen was born. His aunt nudged him in the side. You got yourself a looker.

Why do you think I married her? he whispered.

Are you talking about me? Delia asked.

I'm always talking about how great you are, honey. He waited until she reached him before he kissed her. I was just saying you're a real beauty.

She blushed a pretty shade of pink. It's nice to finally meet you, Rachel. I do hope you'll enjoy your visit.

I have no doubt I will. Rachel gave her a big hug. I hear you're expecting a little Owen.

In August.

Rachel looked at Johnny. And how do you feel about being a big brother?

Good, Johnny said. I have lots of things to teach him.

I see you're having a boy. Rachel glanced between Owen and Delia and winked.

Well, come on into the parlor and make yourself at home.

Delia helped his aunt out of her coat. Supper will be ready in an hour.

I'll get the horses put away for the night, Owen said.

Can I help? Johnny asked.

Sure. He took Johnny's coat, hat, and mittens off the hooks by the door and waited until Johnny put them on.

Don't get into another snowball fight, Delia called out as Owen opened the door. She looked at Rachel. Those two can stay out there for hours if I let them.

Rachel chuckled.

We'll be good this time, Owen said.

Johnny bent down, grabbed some snow off the porch and threw it at Owen.

In retaliation, Owen collected enough snow to make a snowball and glanced at Delia. Uh...it's just this one snowball. I promise.

Another snowball landed on his back. Delia sighed, even as a flicker of amusement crossed her face.

I'll call you in when supper's ready.

Deal. He closed the door and got ready to throw his snowball at the laughing boy.

<h1 style="text-align:center">C H A P T E R 2 2</h1>

The Happy Ending

So, this is how Owen Russell ended up in Omaha, Nebraska. They say some men are born for greatness, some choose greatness, and some have greatness thrust upon them.

For Owen, he was shoved headlong into it. But he managed quite well and soon earned himself a good reputation as the deputy, though he never did match up to Irving's level of fame.

Irving was very happy in Texas where there were enough outlaws to keep him busy doing what he did best.

In August, Delia gave birth to another blond-haired boy, and after much debate, she finally settled on naming him Carl.

A proud Owen and Johnny promised to make him one of the best fishermen in Omaha.

Last, but not least, Joel did find himself married despite all his efforts to avoid what he deemed a most terrible fate. But that is another story for another day...

ABOUT THE AUTHOR

Norma Iris Pagan Morales was born in Ponce, Puerto Rico. She comes from a very lovable family. Her parents, Juan Jose Pagan Rodriguez, and Digna Morales Figueroa, now deceased, always helped her with her projects as a writer and teaching career.

Norma had three siblings, Adelin Milagros Pagan Morales, Juan Jose Pagan Morales, and Julio Manuel Pagan Morales. Julio Manuel Pagan Morales died on September 19, 1998, and my dear sister Adelin Milagros Pagan Morales died on February 17, 2023.

Norma did all her academic studies in New York City, Puerto Rico, and Canada. She worked in the City of New York Police Department. As an Educator, she worked in New York City Bd. Of Education as an English Teacher, in Puerto Rico Bd. of Education as an English teacher and in the Puerto Rico Army National.

She has teaching certifications for English as a Second Language and Teaching English as a Foreign Language.

She had published seventeen books: Proud of My Puerto Rican Bequest, ¿Porque Soy Boricua? Poemas del Alma, Art in Written Form, A Baffling Short Stories Collection, On Job in the Big Apple, Puerto Rican Soldiers Serving with Pride, Nature's Rage in the Caribbean, Boricua de Pura Cepa, You are the One, The Unfaithfuls, Christopher Columbus, Violence in the City, Poemas Tiernos, Mis Raices, My Little Sister and Two Strangers.